THE
Good
GIRL
PART DEUX

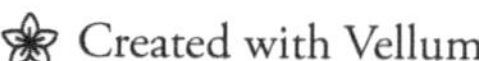 Created with Vellum

THE Good GIRL

PART DEUX

TRACY REED

To my first loves
God
Mommy and Dad

CHAPTER ONE

Gabriella

There was no skirting around the subject. As much as I wanted to keep my relationship with Phillippe a secret, I was outed by a simple text. I gathered up my newfound boldness and repeated my question, "What do you want to know?"

My mother looked at me with a stone face. I looked at her, waiting on her to answer my question. This silent standoff wasn't good. It meant she had several questions for me, and was just figuring out which one to ask first.

I took another long sip from the large white mug she

handed me. The hot coffee was good, but I really needed something solid in my stomach. I looked at the end of the counter and spotted a plate of her fluffy biscuits and strawberry jam.

My mother is an amazing cook. Her eyes remained fixed on me. "Would you like a biscuit?"

Another trick question. If I took the biscuit, she gained the upper hand. If I didn't, she still won because I might pass out from hunger pangs. Last night's dinner had long worn off and I really needed something to fill the hole in my food bank.

I foolishly gave in. "Yes, please." I started to get up.

"No, let me." She walked down to the end of the counter, picked up the plate and jam and placed them in front of me. "Bacon?"

I was definitely being set up. She knew I loved bacon. If I was headed to slaughter, I might as well go on a full stomach. I swallowed hard. "Yes please."

I sliced open a warm biscuit, and piled on some butter and sweet strawberry jam on one half. I bit down and savored the bite. She fixed me a plate with some bacon, eggs and asparagus and placed it in front of me. "Thank you." She went back to her place on the other side of the counter. This torture was nerve-wracking. At least I had something in my stomach. Not that it would help me in my interrogation.

"At what time in the past month did you decide to become a cliché?"

A cliché? I'm not a cliché. A cliché would be me sleeping with my boss to get ahead. On the contrary, if this relationship tanks, I might become the first woman in history to get promoted because she didn't have sex with her boyfriend slash boss.

"I don't understand." That was a lie.

"Let me re-phrase my question. Why are you being an idiot?"

I wasn't being an idiot either. It wasn't like I set out to fall for my boss. It just happened. At least that's the answer I came up with last night while lying in bed.

"I'm not being an idiot."

"Didn't I tell you to make sure being his bed buddy wasn't part of your job description?"

"Yes, but—"

"Did I ask for your commentary?"

What the crap! She asked me a question and now she doesn't want me to answer.

"Gabriella Christina Townsend, have you completely lost your mind?" I wasn't sure if I was allowed to speak or not, so I put another forkful of eggs in my mouth. "What is it about this man that makes you think it's nothing more than an office fling?"

I wasn't sure if this was just an office fling. It could very well end tomorrow, or before I leave for Europe. But I knew I planned on enjoying myself as long as it lasted. For the first time in my life, I was the pretty girl. The girl everyone in the room noticed because I was with the hot guy. So right now, I didn't want to think about the possibility that this relationship could disintegrate at any moment. I just wanted to linger in the haze of adoration that comes with a new relationship.

I swallowed the savory biscuit, wiped my mouth and was prepared to answer her, but my phone started ringing with a familiar ringtone. I reached for it and she snatched it up, looked at the screen and handed it to me.

I didn't need to look at the screen, because I knew who it was. I pressed the Ignore Call button, and stuffed some more eggs and bacon into my mouth. This was going to be a long standoff. In spite of her being upset with me, she still made the best biscuits. I broke off another piece and shoved it into my mouth. Her biscuits reminded me of the ones I had with Phillippe. I took another long sip of the hot liquid to wash down my biscuit and my phone rang again with the same ring tone.

"I know you don't want me to answer it."

I put my cup down, picked up my phone, and pressed the Answer Call button. "Good morning, Mr. Marchant."

"Really?" my mother mumbled as she shook her head. "We're not finished with this."

I went outside, hoping for a little privacy. I exhaled and placed the phone to my ear. "Mon Amour, why are you being so formal?"

"I was talking with my mother and…"

"I understand. I can't wait to meet her."

He wouldn't say that if he knew she was set to castrate him. "I got your text. When will you be back?"

"Not until the end of the week."

"Oh."

"Seems I have to cancel our date."

"I understand."

"Seems we just got started and…"

"Phillippe, it's not a big deal, really."

"But…"

"I understand work comes first.

"No, it's a priority, but you come first."

"Phillippe, I told you, I'm not like the other women you've been with. I don't expect you to feel bad about canceling on me for work, at least not now." I feigned a laugh. "We…this thing is just starting. We don't even know where it's going…if it's going."

"What's that supposed to mean?"

"It means, we've only been on one date."

"Officially." One date and it's already causing problems. "Mon Amour…"

"Yes."

"What's wrong?"

"Nothing." I sighed.

"Okay." He cleared his throat. "I have a list for you."

"A list?"

"Yes."

"So I take it I'm now speaking with my boss?"

"Exactly, Miss Townsend."

Phillippe

I looked out the window while processing the first part of my conversation with Gabriella. When I put her in the car last night, she was fine. If it hadn't been for this crap with Seattle, I wouldn't have sent her home when I did.

Considering her confession about not trusting herself to be alone with me, maybe it was a good thing we ended the evening a little early. Maybe that's why she sounded upset. It wasn't my intention to end our date so early, but it couldn't be helped.

I'm not going to push her, but this is not the way to start a relationship. Maybe I should call her back. I picked up my phone and started to text her.

"What's up man?" Tony asked.

I sighed staring at my phone. "I uhm…"

"What's wrong?"

I laid my phone down, sipped my coffee and exhaled. "I'm not quite sure."

He sat down, poured a cup of coffee, looked at me, opened the top folder and asked, "How's Gabby this morning?"

"Why did you ask me that?"

"Weren't you with her last night?"

"How did you…"

"We've been friends a long time, and when you all but threatened to kill me if I disturbed you last night with anything less than death, I knew what that meant."

I smiled and shifted in my seat. "Was I that obvious?"

"Yep. So how was your evening?"

"Dinner was great." I felt like a teenage boy replaying

my date with the hottest girl in school. "We ate at the restaurant."

"Private room?"

"Of course. Chef Paul really out did himself last night."

"And?"

"She was impressed." I thought back to her reaction when she saw me enter the dining room with the plate of appetizers.

"So, what's the problem?"

"Last night, we…I mean…I didn't realize how difficult it would be to be around her and not be privy to more."

"More?"

"You know, more."

It took him a second and then he smiled. "So the snake wanted out of the box last night?"

"In the worst way possible. You should have seen her. She had on this sexy black dress fitting every curve, and her parfum was everywhere. I wanted to cancel dinner and go straight to dessert, at my place." I smiled.

He nodded. "So what happened?"

"You called."

"I'm sorry, but…"

"I was angry you called and interrupted dinner, but at the same time, I was glad." I got up and started pacing and wringing my hands. "I'm not sure if I can do this."

"I was afraid of this."

"What?"

"You, in love."

"Love? Who said anything about love?"

"I'm sorry. Did I misread the situation? Because from

where I'm sitting, it's clear to see you're in love with this woman."

"I…I'm uhm…where is this coming from?"

"Let's see. Not that you need to tell me everything that's going on in your personal life, but explicit instructions not to contact you unless it was life or death." He shook his head. "Not to mention you've become celibate."

"Celibate? Who said anything about…"

"I know Gabriella very well, remember?"

"But how would you know she's…"

"I'm good at my job. Plus you told me she said she wasn't like the women in your past. No offense bruh, but your past is sprinkled with a cast of very open women. Gabriella is a good girl and she ain't giving up the goodies without a ring and parchment. So is that why you're torn?"

"What are you talking about?"

"Does your plan include marriage? Is that why you're having problems?"

"First of all, my becoming celibate…"

"So you are celibate?"

"I choose to look it as a body fast."

"A body fast?" He shook his head laughing. "I like that."

"Anyway, this body fast, is…who said anything about marriage?"

"Look at you. She's got you all twisted."

"More like tied up in knots." I plopped down in my chair and shook my head.

"I don't believe what I'm witnessing. The wild man has been tamed by a petite ball of curves in less than a month."

"As if I wasn't already having challenges. She says it's not me she's concerned about, it's her."

"You lost me."

"After dinner, we were dancing and really getting to know each other when you called about Seattle. I explained I needed someone there to oversee things, and she suggested you."

"That's what I said."

"I know, but she also said she wanted you to travel with us. She said she felt more comfortable having you with us."

"Why?"

"Because she doesn't trust herself to be alone with me." I smiled.

Tony started choking and patting his chest. "She said what?"

"She said as hard as we may try to not let anything happen, something might happen."

"What did you say?"

I looked at my best friend sitting on the edge of his seat. "Before I knew it, the words came flying out of my mouth. 'Nothing will happen that we don't want to happen.'"

"What?" He leaned back in his seat with his mouth wide open. "What did she say?"

"She just smiled. Now this morning, she's all formal and distant."

Tony stood up and started pacing. "Okay, we've got a problem."

"You think? I've never been in this position. I'm trying to be cool, do as you said, let her call the shots, and keep the snake in the box. But her making this confession makes me think...I didn't sleep at all last night. Her words and that hot body of hers kept invading my thoughts. Just when I thought I was about to get some sleep, she appeared in my dreams in that black dress, doing things that I don't think she..."

"You've got it bad."

"You think? I'm about to spend two weeks in Europe with my girlfriend who has confessed she's not sure she can be trusted to be alone with me. Oh yeah, and I'm celibate."

Tony walked over to the bar and filled two glasses half full, and handed me one of the glasses. "Drink up."

"Are you insane, it's not even noon."

"It's five o'clock somewhere." We both downed the brown liquid in one shot. "We need a plan."

We sat silent for a few minutes. I rubbed my forehead. "Maybe I should cancel the trip. Or leave her at home."

"You can't do that."

"Why not? I'm the boss."

"You need to know what's going on with those leases. Plus, if you want me to get a team on the international expansion, we need that additional space locked up asap. You can't do all of that research on your own. You need the help. Especially since I'll be in Seattle."

"I could ask my cousin to come."

"And have him hit on Gabriella the entire time."

"She's not his type."

"That's what you said." He tilted his head and smiled.

I stood up and started pacing again. "My dad warned me this day would come."

"What day is that?"

"The day when a woman would enter my life and cause a tsunami." Tony laughed at me. "He just failed to mention she'd penetrate my heart and mind while doing it. I'm so screwed."

"Yes you are."

CHAPTER TWO

Gabriella

I haven't slept well the past few nights. Every time I close my eyes, I'm plagued with images of Phillippe. It wouldn't be so bad if the images were of him doing something boring like conducting a meeting or something else work-related. No, these dreams are very salacious, starring the two of us. Honestly, I think I would have been better off not confessing I didn't trust myself to be alone with him.

Even now, if I close my eyes, I'm sure he'll be there in bed on top of me, kissing me and doing things I've only read about in books. I wonder how he looks naked? When he's pressed up against me, I feel every detail of his body and it's like hugging a finely chiseled marble statue. And his hands, my God, his hands are huge.

I really noticed his hands on our first date when they slid down my back and grabbed my behind, they seemed to…uhm… What is wrong with me? These thoughts are not quite pure, and are definitely making it more difficult to be on this long flight alone with him.

I closed my eyes and licked my lips remembering the last time he kissed me, and how he tasted. I felt a smile rise on my lips and my body temperature soared. I wrapped my arms around myself sinking deeper into my fantasy.

"Miss Townsend…Miss Townsend…."

A familiar voice was invading my fantasy followed by a soft nudge. "Oh…" I jumped.

"I'm sorry. Did I startle you?" Gil asked.

"Uhm…no. I'm fine."

"Mr. Marchant called. He's on his way."

"Okay."

"Can I get you something?"

"A glass of ice water would be perfect. Thank you." I sat down.

"I'll be right back."

As quickly as he disappeared, he reappeared and placed the glass on the table in front of me. "Thank you."

"You're welcome. Can I get you anything else?"

"No."

He looked at his watch. "Once we get on the way we'll have a light snack, and dinner a little later."

"I'm sure whatever you have planned will be fine." I

looked around. "Gil, everything seems different. I mean the plane seems larger, or am I imagining it?"

"No Miss, you aren't imagining it. Mr. Marchant and Mr. Walsh took the other jet to Seattle. This is the one we use for international travel."

"Oh."

"It has sleeping quarters with showers and a slightly larger galley."

"Sleeping quarters?"

"Yes. You will be in the front bedroom and Mr. Marchant will be behind you."

"I see. And you?"

"I never sleep," he teased. "But if I get tired, there's a space for me as well. If you'll excuse me."

"Thank you, Gil."

"You're welcome. I'll be in the back if you need anything." He was gone again.

I picked up the glass. The ice cold water was just what I needed to cool down. I laid my head back, closed my eyes, and said a little prayer. I needed to keep alert and not yield to temptation. I slowly nodded off and drifted to that place where Phillippe was the star of my dreams.

Suddenly, the kiss I was dreaming about seemed very real. His lips were just as I remembered the last time we kissed. I tried to smile, but I couldn't. I forced my eyes open, and staring at me was the star of my dreams.

"Mon Amour, you looked so peaceful I thought about not waking you until after takeoff." He gently brushed my cheek. "Miss me?"

I shrugged my shoulder. "Maybe." He clutched his chest

and dropped his head. I lifted his chin and was presented with a beautiful smile, and those incredible dimples. "Maybe I missed you a little." I smiled.

He pressed his lips against mine, and a surge traveled from my lips down my body. He pulled back and whispered, "I missed you too." He stood up. "Did you get settled into your room?"

"No."

He extended his hand to me. "Come, let me show you where you will be sleeping." I stood up and followed Phillippe down to the door on the left, and he pushed it open.

I looked around and it was just like the rest of the jet, champagne and black with hints of brass. And on the bed was a Brockman's garment bag. "What's that?"

"I stopped at Brockman's to pick up some things, and Cameron told me the suit you wanted was on sale." He sat on the side of the bed and pulled me down onto his lap. "Why didn't you get the suit when you got the dress?"

"Because I couldn't afford it."

He brushed the side of my face. "My sweet, if there's something you want…"

"Phillippe, you don't have to…," I dropped my head.

"What's wrong?"

I looked at him, thinking about what I wanted to say. "Thank you, but I wasn't raised to…"

He grabbed my chin. "I didn't mean to imply…I…this is different for me as well."

"You?"

"Yes, I'm not used to having a girlfriend..." I started smiling. "Did I say something amusing?"

I shook my head. "Girlfriend."

"Yes, girlfriend."

"It sounds strange."

"What is strange about what I said?"

"I thought men like you...never mind. You were saying?"

"I'm not used to having a girlfriend that doesn't expect things from me."

"I expect things from you."

"Let me rephrase it. I'm not use to having a girlfriend that doesn't expect a lot of material things from me. So it's going to take a while for me to get used to..."

"Giving yourself?"

"Exactly." He looked at the bag and back at me. "If you want me to return the suit..."

"How about this. We'll work out a payment plan." He started laughing at me. "What's so funny?"

"You." He pulled me closer. "Let's call it a bonus."

"A bonus?"

"You've been working with me over a month and this is my way of saying how much I appreciate the job you've done so far."

I looked at him smiling, and knew I was falling deeper down the rabbit hole. "Okay."

"Good. Now that we have settled that, will you enjoy your bonus?"

"Yes. Thank you."

"Tell you what, since I had to break our date..." I

quickly covered his mouth with my hand. He reached up, pulled my hand down and kissed my palm. "What are you doing?"

"Gil might hear you."

"He knows."

"Oh great, he probably thinks I'm some tramp trying to sleep her way up the corporate ladder."

"He doesn't think that. In fact, he said if this doesn't work out, he'd like to introduce you to his son," he teased.

"Not funny." He kissed me.

"I thought it was best to tell him about us, so he didn't think I was sexually harassing you when he saw me kissing you. You should have seen the look on his face when I told him to make up both bedrooms."

"What did he say?"

"He said, it was about time I dated a lady." My face felt hot. "So no sneaking into my room tonight." I playfully socked him. "Seriously, I told Cameron…"

"I'm not letting you…"

He put his finger against my lips. "Cameron is now your personal shopper."

"I don't need—"

"Yes, you do. With our being on the road a lot, you might not be able to get into the store, and I don't want you to miss out on something you want. When something you like goes on sale, he'll put it aside for you. Or, if you need something sent to you, he can do that as well."

"I…" A knock on the door interrupted our conversation.

"Sir…"

"Yes, Gil?"

"We're ready."

"Thank you. We'll be right there." I started to get up and he pulled me back. "What's wrong?"

"Nothing."

"Are you upset with me?"

"Yes and no. I don't…"

"You don't have to use Cameron, but he's there if you need him." He lifted my chin. "Mon Amour, let's not fight. I didn't mean to overstep my bounds. Forgive me?"

I put my arms around his neck and kissed him. "Yes."

The past week has been hell. Not exactly the best time to start a new relationship, but is there ever really a good time? Having Gabriella in my life gives me something to look forward to. She's forcing me to relax, which doesn't make any sense, because I've never wanted or needed an escape from work. I enjoy what I do. But, but she makes me think there's more to life, or that I'm missing something.

However, the past couple of days, she hasn't sounded like her normal upbeat self. Funny, it was me that was a little apprehensive about mixing business with pleasure, and now it seems like it's in reverse.

I walked into Brockman's surveying everything. I had just enough time to handle a couple of things before heading to the airport. I took over the conference room for a quick meeting.

"Hi, Cameron." I shook his hand.

"Hello, Mr. Marchant."

"Have a seat. I wanted to talk to you." I looked at my watch. I wanted to be at the airport when Gabriella arrived, but it doesn't look like that's going to happen.

"Is there a problem?"

"No. You're an excellent Personal Shopper or, what are we calling your department now?"

"VIP Services."

"I don't really like that. All of our customers are VIPs. You will need to come up with something else."

"Excuse me, sir?"

"I'm offering you the position of Senior Director of Client Services, or whatever it's going to be called."

"Excuse me?"

"I'm sorry. Normally, I would have this meeting in my office. However, I'm running late. I should have been at the airport an hour ago. I'm promoting you. Peter speaks highly of you, and I agree you would be an excellent department head."

"Thank you, sir." We shook hands.

"Phillippe."

"I'm sorry."

"I have been meaning to call to tell you how much I liked the dress you selected for my assistant."

"She's lovely. It was a pleasure working with her."

"About that."

"Yes?"

"With your new position, you might need to scale your client list down. Don't worry, your salary will be more than commensurate."

"Thank you. I'll take care of that immediately."

"However, I want you to personally handle Miss Townsend."

"Yes, sir. I mean Phillippe."

"I like that black dress you selected as well."

"I wish I could take credit, but that was her selection." He smiled. "She's a delight to work with."

"Whenever she comes in, you are to use my discount."

"Oh?" His eyebrows raised.

I understood the shock on his face. My discount is only for my immediate family. My offering it to Gabriella said a lot about our relationship. I didn't even let Chantal use it. I gave her the standard employee discount.

"I should explain…she and I are…"

He looked at me and smiled. "I understand. If you don't mind my saying, she's not like Miss Myers. She would email me photos from the collections immediately after the shows, demanding expedited delivery."

"I had no idea. Well, Miss Townsend isn't like that."

"No, she isn't. And if you don't mind my saying, she has an incredible figure."

I smiled, thinking about Gabriella's curves and how I

couldn't wait to have her in my arms. "Yes, she does." I looked at my watch. "I'm sorry, but I need to get to the airport." We stood up and shook hands.

"Thank you, sir."

"I'll have your new paperwork forwarded tomorrow. Now, if you'll excuse me…"

"Sir, I mean Phillippe, before you leave. I was going to call Miss Townsend later today. The suit she wanted has been marked down and I don't want her to miss out…"

I looked at my watch. "Get it, and I'll take it with me."

———

I boarded the plane, and Gabriella looked so peaceful. She was sleeping and had a slight smile on her face. I didn't want to wake her, but I desperately wanted to kiss her. She's that piece that's been missing from my life.

I handed Gil the garment bag, walked over, and gently pressed my lips against hers. She slowly opened her eyes and greeted me with a smile.

"Hey…"

"Mon Amour…did you miss me?"

Gabriella

Instead of going to London first, Phillippe reversed the schedule. We went to Paris first.

As we drove to the hotel, my nerves started gathering. I was in the city of love with my boyfriend. A man I have been having impure thoughts, fantasies and hot dreams about. *God, please don't let me lose control.* I can't say regret, because let's be real, if something did happen, I doubt I'd regret it. I'd feel really bad, but, man what a memory I'd have.

I looked at Phillippe and smiled.

"Why are you sitting all the way over there?" He grabbed my hand and pulled me next to him. He wrapped his arm around me, rubbing my shoulder.

"It's so beautiful, and this is where you grew up?"

"We divided our time between the city and my grandparents place in Bordeaux."

"Wow. I couldn't imagine not living in the city. Each building is more amazing than the next."

"Let's switch."

"What?"

"Sit here." He climbed over me and I slid closer to the door with a better view of the city. As we made our way into the city, Phillippe pointed out buildings and sights giving me a mini tour.

"It's all so beautiful."

Suddenly, the tour came to an end and we stopped at a beautiful building. "We're here." Phillippe got out of the car, walked around and helped me out while the driver handled the luggage. I looked up staring at the beautiful building. It looked like something out of an art book…grey, gothic details, and an amazing black metal and glass door.

"Wow." I tried not to sound like a tourist, but everything I said gave me away.

He took my hand and we walked inside. I looked around and it looked like a grand mansion. The walls were black lacquer, with incredible art and antiques, mixed with contemporary furniture, beautiful flowers and funky, soulful music. It reminded me of Phillippe…classic, with a little contemporary edge.

I looked around for the check-in desk, but never saw

one. We bypassed all the lobby action and went to an elevator. That's when it occurred to me this might not be a hotel. Maybe we're meeting the realtor before going to our hotel. We rode up to the top floor and the elevator opened directly into the space. I looked around and the view was incredible.

"Where are we?"

Phillippe took off his jacket and placed it on the sofa. He turned and looked at me. "Make yourself comfortable."

I put my bag down, took off my jacket, and handed it to Phillippe. "Where are we?"

"Phillippe…"

A petite woman appeared. "Marie."

"Comment était votre voyage?"

"Our trip was perfect. Merci." He looked at me. "This is Mademoiselle Townsend."

"Plaisir de vous rencontrer." Marie extended her hand to me.

"Pardonnez-moi, je ne parle pas bien Français. That's the one phrase I made sure to learn." I smiled. "Plus I got a translation app."

She smiled. "Forgive me. It is a pleasure to meet you. I apologize. Monsieur did mention that to me. I will try to speak only English."

"No, please…maybe while I am here you can teach me French."

"Oui, je peux le faire…until then, I will use English."

"Merci." I smiled.

"Bien." She smiled. "Come with me and I will show you to your room."

"My room?"

"Oui."

"Excuse me." I turned to Phillippe. It was time to play the girlfriend card. "What is she talking about? I thought we were staying at a hotel."

"Mon Amour, I…"

"Phillippe, I'm not going anywhere until you tell me where we are, and what is going on."

"Un moment Marie, merci."

"Oui."

"Where are we?" I folded my arms in front of my chest.

He stepped closer. "You said you didn't trust yourself to be left alone with me."

"That's not what…Phillippe, tell me where we are, or I'm headed to the nearest Holiday Inn or whatever they call it here."

He smiled. "I'm sorry. I should have told you."

"Told me what?"

"This is my apartment."

"Your apartment?" I looked around and back at him. "Is this why you told me you would handle the hotel in Paris?"

"Yes. I knew if I told you we would be staying at my apartment, you would stress out or not come."

"This is my job. So I wouldn't not come. I probably would have made…"

"I see I have upset you."

"How many other women have stayed here?" He was silent. "I meant what I said Phillippe. I'm not sleeping with you."

"Where did that come from?"

"I don't know…maybe because we're standing in your apartment…in Paris."

He crushed his lips against mine, and his tongue pushed past my tight lips, inside my mouth, shattering my defenses. My hands reached around his neck as he pulled me closer to his chest, and I slowly relaxed. His hands slid down my back pulling me deeper into his space, and at that moment I didn't care where we were. All I wanted was more of his lips and body pressed against mine. He slowly pulled back, brushed his thumb along my bottom lip and smiled, hypnotizing me with his dimples.

"I'm sorry, I should have told you we would be staying here. I thought you would be more comfortable here with Marie than alone in a hotel."

"Oh." I bit my bottom lip.

"I understand your apprehension. But I told you, nothing will happen that neither of us wants to happen."

"So, where are we?"

"My building."

"Your building?"

"This building belongs to my family."

"Your family?" This is the first mention of his family having money. I thought he only owned the restaurant. "Why do I get the impression there's something you're not telling me?"

"What are you saying?"

"The restaurant, now this building…what's going on?"

"I inherited some money and property when my father died."

"Uh-huh."

"You don't believe me."

"I didn't say that."

"Then why does it feel like you don't?"

"Phillippe, your finances aren't my business."

"But…"

"Let me finish. I hope that as we get to know each other, you'll feel comfortable enough to tell me what's going on."

"I'm telling you the truth about the building."

"I believe you about the building, but I know there's more to it."

"Mon Amour, I…"

I held up my hand. "The next time we talk about this building and the restaurant, you better be prepared to tell me whatever it is you're not telling me. Tu comprends?" He looked surprised at my response.

"Oui."

"Where's Marie? I'd like to freshen up."

"Marie." As quickly as she disappeared, she reappeared. "Please show Mademoiselle to her room, Merci."

"This way, Mademoiselle."

I started to walk away and he grabbed my hand. "Do I get a kiss?"

"No." Marie winked at me.

I barely dodged that bullet. I have to remember Gabriella is very perceptive. I just knew I was going to have to come clean about everything when she asked about the apartment. I need to get through this trip and back to the states without her finding out the truth.

———

I tried to sleep, but every time I closed my eyes, Gabriella was there. It would be so easy to go downstairs to her room and make love to her. The hold she has on both my conscious and sub-conscious is overwhelming. I have never been involved with a woman like her. The kicker is, we aren't even sleeping together, and yet she's controlling me.

Her hold on me would make sense if we were physically involved, but we aren't. All we've done is kiss. And, as my grandmother used to say, no inappropriate touching either. Although God knows, I would love to have her full breasts in my hands and feel her nipples brushing against my tongue. When I kiss her, the way she feels pressed against me, sends a charge straight to my...I am running out of things to think about to squash the arousal she ignites in me.

I wonder what she sleeps in? Is it a little frilly gown or pajamas? It's probably something utilitarian, like a long cotton gown. Whatever it is, in my mind, she's naked and the sheet is barely covering her beautiful caramel colored body. She's lying on her stomach with the crisp white sheet just resting at the apex of her curvy behind. And when she turns over, her full breasts are swollen and ripe, just begging for my attention. Her hair is scattered on the pillow, and she has a beautiful smile on her face as a result of the delightful dream she's having.

I climbed out of bed and went down to the gym. I needed to release the lust I was feeling. When I went back upstairs, I was still worked up. I walked down the hall and stopped at Gabriella's door. I placed my hand on the knob and thought one little look to confirm my fantasy might help me sleep. I turned the knob and started to push the door open and stopped.

She's not like the others. She's different. You want this one to last. You can go the distance. You can be the man she thinks you are.

I cursed into the towel, went upstairs to my room, took an ice cold shower and went to sleep.

CHAPTER FOUR

Gabriella

I walked into the kitchen and the incredible smells of French cooking traveled up my nose. I'm not sure who Marie is, but I know she and Phillippe have a special bond.

"Bonjour, Marie."

She looked up and smiled. "Bonjour, Mademoiselle Gabriella."

"Please, just Gabriella." She didn't seem happy with my request. "When it is just us, Gabriella will be fine, s'il vous plaît."

She smiled and nodded. "The other demoiselle was…"

"The other?"

She lowered her head and said something under her breath in French and then looked up at me. "The demoiselle that..."

"Chantal?"

"Oui. Elle n'était pas très plaisante. I'm sorry. I forget, only English." She winked.

"Merci."

She smiled. "We must begin your French lessons today. Monsieur Phillippe loves speaking in his other language."

"He does?"

"Oui." I sat down and she placed a large cup and saucer in front of me, and filled it with coffee. Then she placed a basket of croissants in front of me, along with butter and apricot jam. "Eat, I made this morning."

I took a croissant out of the basket and it was still warm. I broke it in half, spread a little butter and jam on it, and bit down. It was flakey, light and oozing with flavor. It was definitely not like those poor imitation croissants back home. "Marie, this is incredible."

"I have to teach you how to make." Her French accent was beautiful and I appreciated her speaking in English.

"S'il vous plaît." I swallowed the delectable pastry and followed it with a sip of coffee. I've only been in Paris a few hours and my tastebuds are spoiled. "Mademoiselle Chantal?"

"I don't think she really care about Monsieur Phillippe. She only care about the money. When they come, deliveries, all the time they are here, deliveries...Dior, Chanel, Saint

Laurent, Gucci, Vivier, Lanvin, LaPerla, Vuitton, Nina Ricci…they all make deliveries."

"Really?"

"Monsieur Phillippe like nice things, but all she do is shop, shop, shop. She hurt him in the end."

"How?"

"Bonjour." Phillippe walked in, kissed me and then he kissed Marie on the cheek. "How did you sleep?" He walked back and stood next to me.

"Well. How about you?"

"I had a little difficulty falling asleep."

"If you want to stay in today, we…"

He wrapped his arm around me and pulled me to his side. "No. I promised you three days of fun."

"Are you sure, because I can…"

"Are you trying to back out on me?" he smiled.

"No, but if you're tired, we can start our three days tomorrow."

"Are you kidding? This is Paris. There's too much to see."

"Okay. So what do you have planned for today?"

"After breakfast, we are going to the Louvre, then lunch and do a little shopping."

"Shopping?"

"Of course! It's Paris! You come here for the food, the museums and the fashion."

"I'll only agree to the shopping, if you promise not to buy me anything."

"No."

"No?"

"We discussed this."

"Excusez-moi." Marie said as she started to walked away.

"Marie, arrête." Whatever he said made her stop moving. "You are my girlfriend, and you will not stop me from buying you gifts." I folded my arms across my chest. We were at an impasse. He rubbed my arms. "I'm sorry. Why won't you let me buy you anything? It's only money."

"It's not about the money."

"Then what is it?"

"Fine, if it makes you happy, we'll go shopping." I started to walk away but he grabbed my hand and pulled me back into his space. "Mon Amour, what is it?"

"I'm not a whore or some poor waif." I saw the shocked look on Marie's face when I made that statement. She quietly walked out of the kitchen.

"Who called you a whore? "

"No one. I just don't…I don't want you to think I'm some whore stringing you along to get things, or some poor girl just looking to get ahead. And I'm definitely not a cliché, even though I'm dating my boss."

"First, let us address the whore comment. Did your mother call you a whore, is that why you have been a little distant?" I lowered my head. "Mon Amour, look at me."

I raised my head and felt the tears gathering in my eyes. "She said I was being a cliché."

"A cliché?"

I wiped the tear that escaped my eye. "She said you only want me as your bed buddy." He exhaled and gritted his teeth. "And, that once you seduce me…"

"Did you tell her what we discussed?"

"No."

"So where did the whore comment come from?"

"Cliché…whore…a woman who does anything to work her way up the corporate ladder."

He smiled and brushed the tear rolling down my cheek. "I know what a whore is, and you are definitely not a whore, or a cliché." He sighed. "Is this why you don't want me to meet your parents?"

I nodded. "Partly."

"Now, let's address your other comment. Poor waif? Do I make you feel like that?"

I felt another tear sitting on my lower lid. "Sometimes I think you think I'm a little naive."

He gently brushed the side of my face and caught the tear that escaped my eye. "I'm sorry. It's just, in the past, the women I was with were a little…they gravitated to certain things and expected me to provide them."

"I told you. I'm not like the other women."

"I thought that was your way of telling me you're a virgin." He smiled.

"It was, but I also meant I'm not with you because you can buy me things or take me places. I am with you because I like you. I want to get to know you."

"Me, too."

"You're a virgin?" I smiled.

"No." He smiled and kissed me. "I'm sorry. I didn't mean to offend you. This is new for me. So I need you to be patient." I nodded. "Forgive me in advance if I slip up and buy you a gift or three." He brushed the tear away on my cheek. "Okay?"

I nodded. "Okay."

"There is one thing I really want to do, and I'm not taking no for an answer."

"What is it?"

"I'm taking you to Chanel and buying you a little something."

"Phillippe…"

"No. You will not leave Paris without a little something from Chanel."

"You really want to do this?"

"Oui."

"Très bien."

I finished my coffee while Gabriella finished getting ready.

"Je l'aime."

I looked up at Marie. "I like her too."

"Huh."

"What is that supposed to mean?"

"Vous êtes dans l'amour."

I almost choked on my coffee. "I am not in love." I wiped my mouth.

"I see the way you look at her." She topped off my coffee. "How was your late night work out?"

"How do you…"

"I saw you in the hall last night."

I tossed my head back, exhaled, and then looked at Marie. "I don't know what it is about her. I close my eyes and she's there. It's like I can smell her parfum everywhere, even when she's not around. I can deal with her in my mind, but it's the dreams. She's there doing and saying things and…I thought if we stayed here, it would be easier, but…"

"So what were you going to do once you entered her room?"

"I don't know."

"Lie."

"Tu me prends pour un menteur?"

"Not a liar. Just lying to yourself. How do you feel about her? Until you admit how you really feel about her, you are going to have more restless nights."

"You've been talking to Tony."

"Antoine is a smart man, you should listen to him." She picked up the empty plate. "Mademoiselle Gabriella is not like the last one you brought here."

"I know."

"I know you do. And that is why she is staying up here, and not downstairs in the guest apartment."

"That is not the reason."

"Really?" She smiled.

"I did not think…I felt she would…we are also here on business and…"

"All the more reason your employee should be in the guest apartment. You are in love."

"Attends une minute, what were you doing up at two o'clock?"

"Checking on you."

"Moi?"

"Oui. Antoine suggested I keep an eye on you."

"He did?"

"I asked him why, and he said once I observed the two of you, I would understand his request."

"Meaning?"

"Opening that door would have been detrimental to your destiny."

"What does that mean?"

"It means you made the right decision."

CHAPTER FIVE

Gabriella

The day seemed like a fairytale. It felt like I was in a French film. I apologized to Phillippe for flying off the handle like I did. I think my mother's words affected me more than I knew.

After the morning at the Louvre, we had lunch at this amazing bistro. The food was incredible and the wine was spectacular. I think Phillippe plied me with wine so I would be a little more affable when we got to Chanel. I hate to admit it, but his plan worked.

He said I couldn't leave Paris without a little something

from Chanel. What he failed to mention was that he wanted me to spend the afternoon trying on clothes and modeling for him. It all felt very decadent. Phillippe has a friend who works in Public Relations at Chanel, and she arranged for us to tour Coco Chanel's apartment. I'm not a big fashion girl, but stepping back in time like that was amazing. Knowing he went out of his way to do something so generous, impressed me.

I was very pleased he kept his word, and only bought me a little something…a pair of earrings and a compact mirror. To mend things with my mother, I bought her a pair of earrings. The perfect little somethings from Chanel to commemorate my first trip to Paris.

When we returned to the apartment, I went to my room to freshen up. When I opened the door, I noticed a few familiar things from my afternoon at Chanel. The black suit and black cocktail dress I tried were lying on my bed. Along with a gorgeous large, black classic handbag, and a small black and gold evening bag. I was speechless. I tried not to think about the money, although I knew Phillippe had spent several thousand dollars…I mean euros.

I immediately went searching the apartment for him. I found him in the living room reading the paper. I tried to contain my emotions. I stood in front of him with my arms crossed in front of me, tapping my foot.

I cleared my throat and he looked up and put the paper down. "Oui?"

"I thought you said all I needed was a little something from Chanel."

"That is correct."

"I thought we agreed the compact and earrings were the little something."

"That is also correct. They are a little something."

"Then what is that on my bed?"

He stood up, uncrossed my arms, wrapped his arms around my waist and pulled me close. "That is another little something."

"Babe…"

"Oui…"

"You don't have…I mean…that's a lot of something."

"I know."

"So the trip to Chanel was the thing you mentioned you wanted to do?"

He crushed his lips against mine as he pulled me closer. I wrapped my arms around his neck and gave in to the kiss. Phillippe's hands slid down my back, pulling me deeper into his space. A soft moan passed between us, and I knew I was sinking deeper into a world I wasn't prepared for. He pulled back and brushed his thumb along my bottom lip.

"Please, let me spoil you?" I nodded. "Was that a yes?" He smiled.

"Oui."

"Thank you." He kissed me again. "Do you like your gift?"

"Oui…that dress and suit were my favorites. Merci."

"Avec plaisir." He kissed me. "Now get a nap and then, put on your new dress and meet me here in three hours."

"Where are we going?"

"That's a surprise."

My nap was just what I needed to invigorate me. I put on my new dress and met Phillippe in the living room. I wasn't sure where we were going, but from the looks of the expensive dress I was wearing, it must be amazing. But then again, this was Paris…fashion capital of the world.

I walked up behind Phillippe and tapped him on the shoulder. He turned around and I almost fainted. He looked incredible. I have never met a man that looked like this. My body was doing things on the inside that I had never experienced.

"Wow! You…look…beautiful." He kissed me on the neck. I slowly turned around.

"Mademoiselle Gabriella, you look very French."

"Merci, Marie."

"I don't know if I want to share you with anyone tonight. Maybe we should stay in."

"No," Marie jumped in. "You are taking this beautiful young woman out, and letting her enjoy Paris." She walked over and air kissed me on both sides of my face.

"Mon Amour, let's go." He grabbed my hand and we started toward the elevator.

"Do you have your phone and wallet?" Marie asked.

Phillippe patted his pocket and pulled out his phone. "Phone oui, wallet no. Excuse-moi." He disappeared up the stairs.

Marie stepped closer. "Mademoiselle, he's very nervous and excited." She revealed in a low voice.

"I'm the one who's nervous."

"Oui, but not like him."

"He doesn't picture me as the nervous type."

"Il a hâte de vous impressionner. Please forgive. He is anxious to impress you. Let him."

"Oui." I smiled.

"I have it." He came down the stairs waving his wallet. He took my hand and we headed toward the elevator. "Marie, we will be late. Don't worry about breakfast. We will probably sleep in."

"Excuse-moi."

He smiled at my French comment. "I mean it will be very late when we return and we will sleep through breakfast." He kissed me. "Come, we don't want to be late. Bonne nuit, Marie."

"Bonne nuit."

"Bonne nuit, Marie," I kissed her on the cheek.

"Amuse-toi bien…much amuse."

"Definitely."

I was having difficulty not staring at Gabriella. I lifted her hand to my mouth and gently kissed the back. "You are stunning."

She smiled. "Thank you."

"I hope I didn't offend you with the gifts."

"No. I'm just not used to such extravagant gifts. I come from a world where you work hard and save for the things you want. You asked that I be patient with you. I ask that you be patient with me."

"I will." I sipped my wine. "I don't want you to think I'm ashamed of the way you dress."

"I didn't…"

"I like the way you dress. I especially like that black dress you wore to dinner on our first date."

"You do?"

"Yes. I like the way it hits every curve. It has just the right amount of sexy allure." I winked.

"Phillippe…" She looked shocked by my comment.

"You are a very beautiful woman, and the way you move is breathtaking."

"You're embarrassing me." She sipped her wine.

"I'm being honest. Mon Amour, you are very sexy and I know I'm not the only man who sees that." I leaned over and kissed her neck. I could tell she was a little embarrassed. "Relax, Mon Amour, this is Paris. No one is paying attention to us."

"I'm not used to…" Her smile was contagious.

"I will try to contain myself."

"Merci. What do you suggest for dinner?"

"I hope you don't mind, but I took the liberty of pre-ordering."

"Très bien."

"Seems someone has been studying French." I smiled.

"I want to learn French. Marie gave me a few words and phrases."

"She did?"

"Oui. She said you like speaking your other language." She sipped her wine. "Besides, the next time you say something to me in French in the heat of the moment like you did before, I want to know what I'm objecting or agreeing to." She smiled.

I brushed the side of her arm. "Did you enjoy the Louvre?"

"It was incredible. It's one thing to read about it and see it on the internet. But it's completely different when you see it in person. Now the things I studied make sense." Listening to her talk and seeing the city through her eyes was refreshing. "What do you have planned for tonight?"

"Something very French."

"Really?"

"I thought you might like the Moulin Rouge."

"What?" The smile on her face was all the approval I needed. "Are you kidding?"

"No. I thought you might enjoy it."

"Could the day be any more exciting? I'm sorry, did I say that out loud?" She looked around. "First the Louvre, then Coco Chanel's apartment, shopping at Chanel, dinner at the Eiffel Tower, and Moulin Rouge later…it's like a fairytale." Then she got quiet.

"What's wrong?" She shook her head. "Is it too much?"

"It's…very thoughtful."

I leaned over and kissed her. "You deserve it."

———

I don't know where Gabriella gets her energy. After the Moulin Rouge, we went dancing. It was around three thirty when we finally made it back to the apartment.

I don't think either of us was tired. We only came home because the club closed, and the driver was tired. I would have put him in the back and driven, except I'd had too much to drink. In all the times I've brought a companion to Paris, I have never enjoyed myself as much as I have with Gabriella.

We stepped into the elevator, not looking at each other. I reached for her hand and felt like a scared French schoolboy in the presence of his crush. I stepped closer to her, and she looked at me with those gorgeous brown eyes, biting the edge of her bottom lip. Man, that look was dangerous and she didn't even know she was doing it. The elevator stopped and opened to a partially dark space. The only lights on were the one in the hall near Gabriella's room, and the one at the bottom of the staircase leading to my private rooms.

I wasn't ready for the evening…morning to end, but it was late and we both had had a lot to drink. Mixed with a sea of emotions and the aura of the city, I needed to play it safe. I walked her to her room and stopped next to the door. She leaned against the wall and I stood in front of her. She looked at me with half opened eyes and those full lips begging me to kiss her.

"Did you have a good time?"

"I had an amazing time." She began playing with the buttons on my shirt.

"What are you doing?" I braced my hand on the wall. God, she looks delicious. I kept telling myself, "go to bed, alone" .

"I was wondering if you're going to kiss me good night."

I smiled. We had been kissing most of the evening, but this kiss seemed very dangerous. Almost like the doorway to something more. "Do you want me to kiss you?"

"Only if you want to."

I stepped closer and the heat encircling us was dangerous. I brushed the side of her face. "One kiss?"

I wanted to carry her across the threshold and make love to her all night, but that wasn't an option. However, my body wasn't listening. She dragged her hand along the front of my shirt and I almost cracked. I bit my lip, hoping the pain would break the fog of desire and arousal I was fighting.

She looked up and smiled. "One kiss." I brushed her lip with the ball of my thumb. "Don't tease me."

"Tease you?"

She nodded. "All I want is a simple good night kiss."

"Simple?"

"Oui…" She hummed.

I leaned in closer, slipped my hands around her waist, pulled her to my chest and the swell of her breasts pressed against my body mixed with her parfum. The heat and emotions were intoxicating. I lowered my mouth to meet hers, barely grazing her lips. She slipped her delicate hands around my neck, and pulled me closer as I gently pressed my lips against hers. She was drawing me in, taking control, but making me think I had the control. She pulled me closer to her as she opened her mouth, inviting me to take the kiss further, deeper.

I leaned her back against the wall and invaded her mouth. She tasted like port wine and chocolate. We traded soft moans as we pulled each other deeper into the kiss. My hands slid down her back cupping her behind and she didn't flinch. Instead, she kissed me harder, her mouth and tongue demanding.

I pressed myself against her and she cried out. I could feel her heart beating against my chest and her body was shaking. The kiss started to turn into a passionate war, each of us demanding more. I could barely breathe. My tongue dove deeper inside her hot mouth. I felt a deep moan pass from her mouth into mine, traveling down to my core. I fought off the desire to bust the door down and live out the fantasy that had be plaguing me for the past few weeks.

Her moan grew deeper and familiar as she pulled me closer. I knew what I was feeling, but it didn't seem possible that she was on the verge of…I pulled back and looked at her. She was flushed, breathing hard, and her breasts were swollen. I desperately wanted to fill my mouth with…I looked further down her chest and saw just how aroused she was. Oh my God. Then she sucked on her bottom lip. I tried to move, but I couldn't. My eyes were focused on her swollen breasts. She exhaled and that just made it worse.

She looked sinfully delicious and tempting. I smoothed my shirt and patted my chest. I needed to leave, but I couldn't move. She reached up and grazed my lips with her tongue, before picking up where we left off. I couldn't resist her. She pressed her body against mine, and when my tongue hit the back of her mouth, she cried out and pulled back.

She opened the door and stood in the doorway. For a brief moment, I thought she was going to invite me inside.

"Good night." She closed the door, and I stood there wondering what just happened.

I fell against the wall feeling as satisfied as if I'd just made love for the past few hours. I was breathless, my legs were weak, I was drained, and my body was shaking.

I lifted myself off the wall and started towards the stairs. Suddenly, my phone started vibrating and I looked at the screen.

Gabriella: You didn't say good night.

Is she kidding me? The sub-text in those words could have easily sent me back to her room.

Phillippe: Good night, Mon Amour.

I am in way over my head.

CHAPTER SIX

Gabriella

I rolled over and grabbed my head. It was pounding. I remember everything about last night, except getting into bed. I looked down and saw I was naked. I looked around for my robe and saw it lying on the edge of the bed. I started to climb out of bed, and noticed the silver tray on the bedside table. The smell of fresh coffee traveled up my nose. I reached for the white card and read it out loud.

"Drink some water, then sip some coffee. Eat the croissant, sip more water, take both aspirin, drink more coffee and water.

Wait a few minutes before trying to stand up. Then get dressed and meet me in the kitchen. Phillippe."

I looked down at what I wasn't wearing and hoped he hadn't seen me. I followed the instructions and an hour later I stumbled into the kitchen. The aspirin helped some, but my head was still very angry with me.

"Bonjour, is there any more coffee?" I stood in the doorway holding my head.

Phillippe stood up. My eyes were barely open, but from what I could see, he looked rested. "Bonjour, Mon Amour." He walked over, kissed me and took the tray. "Seems the wine hit you hard."

"Just a little."

"Is this your first hangover?" he teased.

"I am not hung over," I protested.

"My Sweet, when you can barely open your eyes and you've been asleep for," he looked at his watch. "over ten hours, I think it's safe to say you're hung over."

I sat down. "What time is it?"

"A little after two."

"I slept half the day. I'm sorry. We were supposed to continue our museum tour."

He hugged me. "Bébé, it's okay. I've only been up a couple of hours myself."

"*Really?*" I tried to look up, but my eyelashes hurt.

He kissed me. "Really."

Marie walked into the kitchen. "Bonjour Mademoiselle Gabriella. I see you have become very French." She teased.

"Marie, I thought you were on my side?"

"I am." She laughed. "Did you take the aspirin?"

"Oui."

"Care to try some fruit and yogurt?"

"Oui, merci." I rubbed my head.

"Cela a seulement enlevé une nuit pour que vous deveniez très Français."

"English, s'il vous plaît. Merci."

She and Phillippe laughed. "Bébé, she said it has only taken you one night on the town to become très Français… very French." He kissed me on the forehead. "I need to make a call. I'm glad you had a good time last night." He left Marie and me in the kitchen.

Marie placed a cup of black coffee on the counter in front of me. "Did you enjoy yourself?"

"Oui." I sipped my coffee. "Marie, do you…the tray in my room…"

"I did."

I sighed and patted my chest. "I was a little concerned, Phillippe had…I mean we have…"

"Un arrangement."

I didn't need that translated. "Oui. As you heard the other day, we are not sleeping together."

"I know." She continued making me something to eat. "He never has women here."

"What? But you said with Mademoiselle Chantal there were a lot of deliveries."

"True. All packages came here, but she stayed downstairs."

"Like me?"

"No. Downstairs in the guest apartment."

"Guest apartment? I don't understand?"

"Monsieur, never have women stay here." She placed a bowl of berries and yogurt in front of me.

"Merci." I bowed my head and said a soft prayer. "Amen."

"Amen." She smiled. "You are very good for him."

"I am?"

"Oui." She placed a glass of water in front of the bowl.

"You were saying about the other women…"

"Monsieur never let them stay. He always keep them downstairs. If he wanted…to be intimate," I smiled at her trying to be discrete. "He would go downstairs."

"He would?"

"Oui. He never have them here."

"Did he say why?"

"No. I just knew they were not…I know he did not…"

"Mademoiselle Chantal never stayed upstairs?"

"No. She came up for breakfast and one dinner. I didn't like her."

I smiled. "Why not?"

"Grossier, méchant, égoïste." She shook her head frowning. Some words translate very well. "Please forgive."

"I understood what you said."

"She never attempt to speak French, not even merci. She demand we only speak Anglais."

"You're kidding."

"No. That offend him, but you…he smiles and is excited to see you considering him. He says you will be back soon for a visit."

"He did?"

"Oui. I like you. We will be friends."

"I like you, too."

"Don't hurt him."

"I won't."

"And I will make sure he does not hurt you."

"Merci."

"Mange votre petit déjeuner…eat your breakfast."

This morning I got up with a new attitude and thought process for my relationship with Gabriella. Instead of focusing on what she's not giving me, I'm focusing on what she is. I've been so consumed with how to avoid having her in my bed, that I forgot I have allowed her some place no other woman has been…. my mind and my heart.

I suspected she was a little drunk by the way she was acting last night. Or, maybe that's the excuse I prefer to believe. If that was her sober, I'm in trouble.

In my quest to be the perfect boyfriend, with Marie's help I prepared a little morning hangover tray. I knocked on Gabriella's door three times, but there was no answer. I took a chance and went inside. If she was in the shower, I'd leave the tray and disappear.

I stood in the open doorway and looked around the room. The dreadful noise I heard scared me. It wasn't the shower, but Gabriella snoring. How is it possible such a beautiful woman could make such a dreadful sound.

I opened one shade to let in some light and cautiously approached the bed. I almost dropped the tray when my eyes landed on her in bed. I never expected to see what I saw. I thought I was standing in one of my dreams. I swallowed hard and tried not to look, but I couldn't not look. It was the most beautiful site I had ever seen.

In my fantasy, she slept in the nude, but my good sense told me otherwise. My God, the image of her lying on her back, her thick, dark, curly hair spread out on the pillows, and the sheet just below her navel, was breathtaking. My eyes traveled down the center of her body and back up resting on her incredible breasts. It was my dream come to life.

I wanted to crawl into bed on top of her and fill my hands with her beautiful caramel colored breasts. Those perfect hard nipples were staring at me, just begging for my tongue. Then she smiled. Was she awake and teasing me? No. She must have been dreaming, and it had put a sweet smile on her face. Then she rolled over and pushed the sheet down, revealing the deep sway of her full, luscious behind. My mind and body were at war. My mind said leave. However, at that moment, I didn't care that I had let her into my heart, when all I wanted to do was crawl on top of her and…I swallowed hard and forced my body to listen to my mind.

I quietly hurried out, closing the door behind me. I

leaned up against the wall, drank the water, and stood still waiting for my body to return to some sort of normalcy. I wiped my wet forehead, walked back to the kitchen, and placed the tray on the counter.

"Marie, veuillez remplacer, merci." I drank the water without stopping for air. "Encore, s'il vous plaît, merci." This time I drank it in parts.

"C'est tout?"

"Please replace the water and napkin, and take the tray to Mademoiselle's room. Merci." She replaced the items and took the tray back to Gabriella's room. When she returned, she topped off my water. "Was she still asleep?"

"Oui." She looked at me smiling.

"Comment?" My body was still writhing, and sitting down was too painful. I must be out of my mind to have Gabriella here. I should have put her downstairs in the guest apartment. I looked at Marie. "Did you cover her up?"

"Oui." She was still smiling.

"Comment?"

"Qu'est-ce qui s'est passé hier soir?"

"After dinner and the Moulin Rouge, we went dancing."

"You did?" She questioned me with a raised eyebrow.

"Oui, and then nous sommes rentrées à la maison. Don't look at me like that. Nothing happened. I kissed her and went to bed, alone." I drank half of the water.

"You did not sneak into her chambre à coucher?"

"No, I did not go back to her bedroom last night."

She nodded. "And when you were in there, did you touch her?"

"No." I patted my forehead with the napkin.

"But you wanted to."

"Oui, vachement."

"She's beautiful, no?"

"Très, très, très belle."

"This is the first time I see you be intimate with someone."

"Pardon?"

"You are sharing you, and that takes great courage."

"Oui, it does." She filled my glass again.

"That means more to mademoiselle than all the belle dresses in Paris."

"She says she only wants me, not les choses…things."

"She's not like cette fille."

"You're right. She's nothing like Mademoiselle Chantal."

She pointed to her chest. "Elle ne desire que ce qui est à l'intérieur."

"I know. She said she wants to know me."

"Then give her what she wants…you. Tell her everything."

"What if she leaves?"

"She won't."

I walked over and hugged her. "Merci, Marie."

"You are welcome."

Gabriella

I sort of messed up Phillippe's plans for today. Actually, it's his fault for planning such an amazing date last night. He did very well with his rain check.

Instead of going to a museum, we spent the afternoon walking around the city. We looked like all the other French couples or lovers strolling the city.

"Marie likes you."

I looked at him smiling. "I like her, too." He wrapped his arm around my waist and we continued walking. "She says she is going to teach me how to be a French woman."

"Really?" He smiled.

"Oui." He kissed me. "She's been teaching me French."

"Vraiment ?"

"Oui, vraiment."

"You understood what I said?"

"Oui, Monsieur Marchant."

"Soon, tu parleras couramment."

"Maybe by our next trip."

"Next trip?"

"Oui, Marie said you told her we would be back soon."

"Would you like that?"

"Oui, beaucoup."

We stopped walking and he cupped my face in his hands and gently pressed his lips against mine. We stood on the side of the street kissing like some of the French couples I'd seen on our walk. "Merci."

"Pourquoi?"

"Making the effort."

"Je ne comprends pas."

"That sounds so beautiful." He kissed me again. "I love hearing you speak French."

I remembered what Marie said about how he loves speaking French. "I'm trying."

"And I appreciate it." He slipped his arm back around my waist and we continued walking.

"Besides, if we are going to be doing business here, I need to be able to communicate. I want to be an asset, not a liability."

"Liability?"

"If I don't understand the language, I can't help you."

He stopped walking and looked at me. "What did you say?"

"I'm part of your team, and we need to speak the same language. Did I say something wrong?"

"No."

"Plus, Marie says you often slip into your French tongue when you get angry. I'm not going to argue with you without knowing what you're saying."

"She said that?" We laughed and continued walking.

"She also gave me a list of things I need to get."

"A list?"

"Oui, she said now that I have survived my first night out in Paris, I need to become a proper French woman."

"She did?" he smiled.

"Oui."

"And how are you to become a proper French woman?"

I reached into my bag and pulled out the list and started reading. "She said I need a nice bag, Chanel or Dior or Hermes if possible. A good pair of dark jeans and a pair of white jeans, a leather jacket, a beautiful scarf, preferably an Hermes scarf, the perfect black dress, black stiletto pumps, beautiful lingerie, a signature scent, and the perfect red lipstick."

"Let me see that." I handed him the slip of paper. "You don't have most of the things on this list. I guess this mean we're going shopping?"

I tried to take the list back and he raised his hand up so I couldn't reach it. "Give me that." We stopped walking and I tried to jump up and snatch the paper back.

"Not until you answer my question." I stood still,

folded my arms across my chest pouting. "Now you look like a French woman." He smiled. "Answer me, and I'll give the paper back."

"Oui." He kissed me and handed me the slip of paper.

He took his phone out of his pocket, pressed a number and said something in French. He was speaking so fast, I couldn't discern his side of the conversation. He ended the call, placed his phone back in his pocket and kissed me. "Dépêche-toi, nous ne voulons pas être en retard." He took my hand and we continued walking.

"Where are we going?"

"To work on your list."

I stopped walking. "What did you do?"

"You'll see."

I hesitated, but his smile convinced me to trust him. We continued walking and a couple of blocks later, we stopped in front of a boutique. "Where are we?"

"According to your list, you need some lingerie."

I looked at him. "Comment?"

"You have an appointment inside."

"What?"

"This is one of the best lingerie shops in Paris."

My mouth dropped open and I looked at him. "Comment?"

He took my hand and led me inside. "Bonjour, Monsieur Marchant."

"Bonjour, Madame Béatrice." He kissed the older woman on both cheeks. They exchanged words in French so fast I couldn't understand. I looked around at all the beautiful delicate lace and silk underthings. French women really are different. "Mon Amour…"

"Oui…"

"Madame, ma copine Gabriella."

"Enchantée."

"C'est un plaisir de faire votre connaissance. Elle est belle."

"Merci."

"Ah, vous parlez français ?" she asked.

"Un peu." I smiled.

"We will use English."

I looked at Phillippe. "Mon Amour, Madame Beatrice is going to help you."

"Help me?"

"I told her you wanted to get some things."

"Excusez-nous." I waited for her to walk away. "What did you do?" I looked around the store. It was obvious that not only was everything beautiful, it was also very expensive.

"I told her you wanted to get a few things."

"Phillippe…I'm not…" I looked at him and I could see that if I rejected his gift, he'd be upset. "I'll only accept this gift if you leave."

He raised up his hands to surrender. "Agreed." He smiled, took my hand and escorted me back to the older woman. "I gave Madame Beatrice a limit and instructions not to tell you how much."

"Comment!"

"I don't want you to think about the money." He kissed

me. "I will be back in two hours." He turned to Madame Beatrice. "Will that be enough time?"

"Oui, Monsieur."

He kissed me. "A bientôt, Mon Amour." He walked out and Madame Beatrice turned to me.

"Mademoiselle, I see the look on your face. Oui, he has bought for others, but not like this."

"Really?"

"Really." She smiled. "Now let's get started.

Two hours quickly turned into three hours. When Phillippe returned, I had a new lingerie wardrobe, and I have to admit, I did feel a little sexier. French women really know how to embrace their femininity.

I must be out of my mind. I just begged my girlfriend, who I am not sleeping with, to let me buy her a new lingerie wardrobe which I will probably never see. I hope she gets at least one night gown and a robe. Not that it will matter, because every time I close my eyes, I'll see her lying in bed looking like a beautiful, naked angel.

What is happening to me? I walked into the kitchen.

"How was your walk?"

"Oh…I didn't see you, Marie." I walked over to the counter, opened a bottle of water, and took a long swallow.

"I'm sorry. How was your walk?"

"It was nice."

"Where did you go?"

"Nowhere in particular."

"How is Madame Beatrice?"

I almost choked on my water. "Excusez moi?"

"I saw Mademoiselle Gabriella carrying sacs from a certain lingerie shop." She continued washing dishes. "That will not make her change her mind about being intimate with you."

"Je sais."

"If you know, then why do it?"

"She said you told her she needed some lingerie."

"Oui, but you did not have to buy it."

"I wanted to."

"Pourquoi ?"

"I don't know. I just…it excited me to see her smile."

"You didn't need to buy her expensive lingerie to see her smile." She walked over and patted my chest. "Just share your heart and you will always see her smile."

CHAPTER EIGHT

Gabriella

"You seem far away. What's troubling you?"

I leaned back against Phillippe's chest. I think this is the most intimate we've been apart from kissing. I can feel his heart beating and the steady rhythm is calming. I can also feel something else pressing against my behind. I'm trying not to get too close, but the third person in our little day at the park is making it's presence known.

I lifted his hand looking at his long, thick fingers and the vast palm. These are the hands of a strong man. A man that knows what he wants and how to get it. I placed my hand against his and it dwarfed in comparison.

"You have incredibly large hands."

"Is that a good thing or a bad thing?"

I was suddenly reminded of my Aunt Niki's words about the size of a man's hand in relation to the size of a couple of other parts of his body. I looked at Phillippe's feet and they too were extremely large. And judging from the third person at our picnic, I think it was safe to say Aunt Niki's theory might be correct. My mind went to a place I've been trying to avoid, especially while conscious.

"Uhm…depends?"

"Depends?"

"Oui. Depends on the current need."

"Excusez moi?" I tilted my head and looked up at him smiling. "I sense someone is being bad."

"Who me?"

"Oui, vous avec le beau sourire."

"You lost me on that one."

"The one with the beautiful smile."

"Merci." I got back in my spot.

"I want to ask you something."

"Ce quoi?"

He lifted my hand and kissed it. "Don't take this the wrong way and it's not a ploy, just curiosity." I turned to face him. "Why have you decided to wait until marriage to have sex?"

I tucked my hair behind my ear and looked at him. I knew at some point this was going to come up and he'd want a more defined answer. "I uhm…"

"Is it because of God or did something happen?"

"It's because of God. I believe in and love Him, so I choose to follow His word and commands. It's not like he doesn't want me to have sex. He just wants me to share that only with my husband." I looked at him waiting on a response. "I love God first and foremost. Yes, I could have had sex and I know God would have forgiven me, but I don't think I would have forgiven myself."

"You don't?"

"No."

"I don't want to just have sex. I know it may sound like innocent schoolgirl talk, but I want to make love. For me, being in a relationship is serious."

"Me too."

I patted his chest. "I mean, it's not like I've dated a lot, but the few times I have, I've always asked myself, 'Is this someone I could picture myself growing old with? Having babies with? Making love to?'"

He smiled. "And what were your answers when you met me?"

"You're assuming I asked myself questions about you." I smiled.

"You just said…"

How can I say what I feel without it causing a problem. What if my response scares him and ends all of this? "I've been too afraid to let my mind go there."

"Why?"

I dropped my head and then looked up. "I like you, a lot. And I'm scared you're going to discover you can't live without the things I'm not giving you."

He brushed the side of my face, and I felt tears welling up in my eyes. He cupped my face in his hands and pressed his lips against mine. The kiss was gentle, sweet…filled with compassion.

"If I didn't respect your honesty and decision not to have sex, we wouldn't be here."

"It's only been…"

He kissed me again. "I know how long it's been." He smiled. "Granted, I think sex with you would be incredible." I smiled. "However, I agree. I think making love would be so much better."

"But what if…"

"We aren't going to talk about what ifs. We're only going to talk about what is."

"What is?" I teased.

"Oui. Like how is it possible for such a virtuous woman to kiss so passionately?" My face felt hot. "I'm serious. I want to know. Because I have never kissed a woman that kisses like you do. The way you seduce me with your mouth is overwhelming."

"Very funny."

"You don't see it, do you?"

"What?"

"You my sweet, possess a sex appeal and passion so intense, it is indescribable."

I started to get up and he pulled me back down and cupped my face in his hands. "You're right. I think it's best that you don't make love until you are married."

"You do?"

He looked at me smiling. "Oui. Because I heard the way

a woman kisses is the way she makes love." He smiled and raised an eyebrow.

After my conversation with Gabriella today, my thoughts were confirmed. She has no clue as to how she effects me. More specifically, she hasn't got a clue as to how sexy she is, or the amount of passion she possesses.

It was excruciating, yet very pleasurable, having her nestled between my thighs. It took every ounce of self control I had to keep myself in check. Then she started squirming and shifting against me until she found a spot she liked. Thank God, she couldn't see the agony on my face.

It wouldn't be so bad if she was aware of what she was doing and playing a game, but she is genuinely naïve to her body language. I tried not to touch her, but I couldn't resist slipping my hands around her waist and kissing her neck. The soft giggle she makes when I nuzzle her neck makes me laugh.

I understand her reasons and desire for saving herself, and I think it's sweet. It made me think back to my first time with a woman. To be honest, I don't remember much about it. Of course I won't forget it, but I don't have any impactful memories. Maybe that's what Gabriella was talking about.

Her theories on making love verses just sex made me think. I want that. I want to know that kind of love. Part of me envies her, in that when she does make love, it will be impactful...probably very romantic. Now I sound like a school girl.

I read an article about a man who said that his love for God allowed him to make love to his wife on an intense and highly erotic level he had never experienced before. Maybe that's why Gabriella kisses so intensely and is so full of passion. Whatever it is, I want it. I want that kind of passion in my life.

CHAPTER NINE

Gabriella

"Bonjour Monsieur Tony." I got up and double air kissed him.

"Bonjour, Mademoiselle Gabby." He sat down in one of the chairs in front of my desk. "How was your trip?"

"Très magnifique." The smile on my face more than answered his question.

"You look very French."

"Merci."

"Did you and Phillippe get any work done?" He teased.

"Oui." He shook his head smiling. "I'll have the reports finished this afternoon. How is everything in Seattle?"

"We're moving everything this weekend. I'm only here for the day. I go back in the morning."

"I'll get to work clearing Phillippe's schedule for the rest of the afternoon and the weekend."

"Thank you…merci."

"Avec plaisir."

"You look different."

"I do?"

"Oui."

"Marie is teaching me how to be a proper French woman."

"So you met Marie?"

"Oui. I like her."

"Elle est très douce et maternelle."

"Bear with me, I'm still learning… what did you say?"

"She's very sweet and motherly."

"Exactly."

"Did you go to the Louvre?"

"Oui. And the Moulin Rouge, the Eiffel Tower, Notre Dame. We took that dinner cruise on the Seine and wine tasting in Bordeaux."

"Wow! Did you go shopping?"

"Yes, and the food! I ate so much. I can't wait to go back!"

"Go back?'

"Oui. Phillippe wants to meet with the design team once the lease is signed."

"Was the apartment comfortable?"

"Yes, it was amazing waking up every morning with the Paris sunlight warming my face."

"Really. So you…"

The door opened and Phillippe walked in. Phillippe walked over and hugged his best friend. "Hey man, what's up?"

"Mademoiselle Townsend was filling me in on your trip."

He looked at me and smiled. "She was?" Phillippe rubbed my shoulder. "Would you order lunch and…"

"Clear your day…already working on it. And lunch is in your office."

"Thank you." He leaned down to kiss me and I leaned back. "I'm sorry, I forgot."

"What's going on?" Tony asked.

"During business hours, it's hands off."

He laughed. "Since when, because…"

"I told Phillippe, when we're in the office, we have to remain professional." Tony laughed. "Don't laugh. I'm serious."

"Come on, fill me in." Tony walked into Phillippe's office. "Have a seat. I'll be right there." He came back to me. "Gabriella…"

I looked up. "Yes?"

He crushed his lips against mine and I fell back in my chair as he kissed me. He pulled back and winked at me.

Phillippe

I walked into my office, closed the door, and joined Tony at the conference table.

"What was that all about?" he asked as he opened the box with his lunch.

"What?"

"The kiss."

I sat down. "We agreed to keep things professional in the office."

"Uh-huh…I don't think that kiss was exactly professional."

I smiled and rubbed my finger across my bottom lip. "No, it wasn't."

"I'm not going to even ask how your trip was."

"What does that mean?" I opened the box and inhaled the savory aroma of my lunch. The mushroom risotto was today's special at my restaurant.

"It's written all over your face. Not to mention the way Gabby is glowing. Did something happen?"

"If you're asking did we make love, the answer is no. Not that it's any of your business."

He wiped his mouth and leaned back in his chair. "Something happened."

"Will you give it a rest? We had a good time, did a little sightseeing, some shopping, worked and came home." I put a forkful of the mushroom risotto in my mouth.

"Uh-huh…and she stayed in your apartment."

"Who told you that?"

"She did when she mentioned the view." He raised one eyebrow. "I'm very familiar with your place in Paris. I know firsthand that the bedroom in the guest apartment doesn't get any morning sun. That's why I like staying in it."

"Yes, Gabriella stayed in the guest room in my apartment." I ate another forkful of risotto.

"If I'm not mistaken, she's the first woman to do so." He ate a forkful of lasagna.

"Is there something you want to ask me?"

He was silent. "Was the trip a success?"

"Yes, I found some spaces that could work. I'm still waiting on Gabriella's report before…"

"You know that's not what I mean."

I looked at my best friend wondering how much to reveal. Gabriella and I had every intention of keeping our personal relationship private. However, that's a little difficult seeing we work together. Couple that with the fact that my best friend can read me like a book. I had no choice but to answer him.

I filled two glasses with sparkling water and put one in front of Tony. I took a sip and thought carefully about what I was going to say.

"Uhm…it started off a little tense. I really wasn't sure if she was still on board with us."

"I thought you guys were doing this thing?"

"You know how crazy things were before I left. I barely spoke with her and the few times I did, all she wanted to talk about was work and I wanted to talk to her like…"

"Her man."

"Exactly." I sipped my water, wishing it was something stronger, but it was too early in the day. "The days leading up to our trip, she kept brushing me off."

He sipped his water. "Then what happened, because she's all smiles and speaking French."

"We talked. More like she went off on me when I offered to take her shopping."

"What?"

"I should have known better after the suit incident."

"Back up. What suit incident?"

"When I stopped at Brockman's, Cameron gave me a message for her about a suit she wanted. It was on sale, and I got it so she wouldn't miss out on it."

"She chewed you out for buying her a suit?"

"Yes. She has this thing about accepting gifts from me."

"I don't understand."

"She said she doesn't want things from me."

"So, you bought her a suit?"

"Yes." He still looked confused. "I knew she wanted it. So I got it."

"You know what? I'm just going to pretend I understand what you're saying so we can get to work."

"I thought I was being a good boyfriend by buying her something she wanted."

"Uh-huh."

"Strange girl. You know, she offered to pay me back over

time. She said we needed to work out a payment plan." He started laughing.

"Are you kidding?" He laughed.

"No, she was serious. I told her to look at it as a bonus."

"Did that work?"

"Yes. But when I told her I wanted to take her shopping at Chanel, she freaked out and said she wasn't a whore or a cliché."

"What?"

"It all has something to do with her mother and why she doesn't want me to meet her parents yet."

"You lost me."

"Her mother doesn't like me. Can you believe it? I haven't even met the woman, and I'm at the top of her hit list." I sipped my water.

"Are you serious?"

"Not to brag, but I'm a great guy."

"You're kidding me, right?"

"Am I missing something?"

"You my brother, are most women's fantasy, every mother's dream, and every father's nightmare."

"Excuse me?"

"Just look at you. If I didn't know you, I wouldn't let you near my daughter."

"Are you serious?"

"When a parent sees you coming to pick up their daughter, they want to close the door and put their baby girl under lock and key."

"And what about you?"

"Me? Parents just think I'm a well-dressed thug...the

proverbial Bad Boy. Trust me, they aren't too excited to see me either, but I do get invited inside."

"So, it's my fault I haven't met her parents?"

"No. It's theirs. Once she figures out the best time to introduce you, she'll invite you for dinner. Until then, keep doing what you're doing, following her lead."

———

"Hello, Mother." She turned around, and her smile reminded me of the days when I was a little boy coming home from school, excited to share my day with her. She hasn't aged a bit. In my mind, she will always be that beautiful, young mother always dressed for a fancy lunch. Part of me wishes she would find a nice man to date, but the protective son cannot stand the thought of any man other than my father kissing her.

"Phillippe." I walked over, wrapped my arms around her waiting on her gentle kiss on the cheek. "When did you get back?"

"Day before yesterday."

"And why am I just now seeing you?"

"Work?" I posed it as a question hoping she would accept my excuse.

"I think not." She returned to clipping her beloved yellow roses. "I think it has more to do with the young lady you took with you." She looked at me with a raised eyebrow.

"Aunt Hilarie."

"Oui. She said I must be delighted to see you have

finally found a suitable companion." She looked at me with a slight smirk. "Imagine my surprise when I couldn't really comment seeing that I have yet to meet the young woman."

"It was purely coincidental that Aunt Hilarie met Gabriella."

"Is that her name?"

"Oui."

"Hilarie says she's very pretty. What does she do?"

"She's part of my team."

She stopped clipping, and turned to face me. "Am I correct in understanding that you are dating your employee?"

"Not exactly."

"Then what exactly?" I turned away. "Phillippe, look at me." I looked at her and suddenly felt like a five year old boy being chastised for not eating his vegetables.

"It's not what you think."

"How do you know what I am thinking." She put her gloves and shears in the basket along with her roses. I linked her arm through mine and we started walking. "Son, I know your grandfather is putting a lot of pressure on you and…"

"I'm not…"

"Listen to me. I love your grandfather. But he can be a little overbearing, especially when it comes to you."

"I know."

"I appreciate your stepping in at Morgan Grant. However, I don't want you to feel obligated to also take on a wife because he said you should."

I stopped walking. "Where is this coming from?"

"I know he told you he wouldn't make you CEO unless you had a wife."

"I'm not with Gabriella because of grandfather's request."

"You aren't?"

"No."

"Then why the rush?"

"I'm not rushing."

She looked at me and then gently stroked the side of my face. "I'm sorry. I just thought…"

"My relationship with Gabriella has nothing to do with grandfather's request. In fact, she doesn't know about grandfather, or the details of my involvement with the company."

"What did you tell her?"

"I told her the chairman and I met at a party which led to his offering me the position."

"So she thinks…"

"I'm just a guy who inherited a little money from his father."

"And how long do you think that story will hold up?"

"I hope long enough to see where this relationship is going." She nodded and threaded her arm around mine, and we continued walking.

"Tell me about her."

I felt like a nervous teenager talking about his crush. "She's nothing like Chantal."

"I already like her."

"Mother…"

"I'm sorry, but I did not like that brat."

"Seems no one liked her."

"No one?"

"Oui, Marie, Tony, Marcos, Aunt Hilarie, Claudette…
even Cameron."

"That should tell you a lot." I looked at her. "I'm sorry.
Continue."

"Gabriella is…I can't quite explain it. All I know is I feel
calm and peaceful whenever I'm around her. She excites me
in a way no other woman ever has."

"Marie said she stayed in your apartment."

"Oui"

"And that you are not sleeping with her, yet you bought
her a new lingerie wardrobe at Madame Beatrice's and took
her shopping at Chanel."

"Oui."

"So what are your intentions?"

"My intentions?"

"Qu'est-ce que tu préviens?"

"I'm not sure. Right now, my plan is to follow her lead."

"Excuse-moi? Did my son say that?"

I smiled. My mother has a tendency to shift between
English and French when she's excited and shocked.

"I can't believe it either."

We stepped up onto the patio and I waited for her to sit
down. She poured each of us a glass of wine. She took a sip
and looked at me. "I hope I get the opportunity to meet
Mademoiselle Gabriella."

"In time." I sipped my wine and noticed an old card-
board box on the chair next to me. "What's that?"

"Ah, Monique was cleaning out a closet and said this
belonged to you."

"I don't recall leaving a box in a closet."

"Open it." I stood up and opened the box. Sorting through the contents nothing looked familiar until I got to a photo. "Is this father?" I handed her the framed photo.

"Yes. Where did you…"

"When was that taken? He was so young."

She gently brushed her finger across the photo. "This is how I met your father."

"I don't understand."

"I was sitting at a cafe and spotted this beautiful man and felt compelled to take his picture. I remember he came up to me right after I snapped it. He said, 'I hope you got my good side.' I remember his accent was incredibly sexy. I looked at him, and trying to be coy, replied, 'All you have are good sides.'"

"Mother, I can't believe you were that forward."

She took the photo and brushed her finger across the glass. "He was a very handsome man." A sad smile covered her face then she looked at me. "You look so much like him."

I looked deeper into the box and pulled out a black leather book. "What's this?" I took it out, opened it up and handed it to her.

She thumbed through the pages. "Oh my God. I was wondering what happened to this." She placed the book on the table and continued turning the pages.

"What is it?"

"It's your father's prayer journal."

"His what?"

She got up and walked over to the box, digging and

fishing until she pulled out another large black leather book. "Oh, mon Dieu."

"What is it mother?"

She pushed the box aside, placed the large book down on the table and started turning pages. "I have been looking for this." She covered her mouth and I saw tears landing on the pages.

"Mother…"

She looked at me with tear-filled eyes. "This is your father's Bible."

"His what?"

"His Bible."

I don't recall my father being a religious man. I remember when we lived in Paris, we would go to church, but I don't recall him doing anything that would be considered religious. "How did it get into this box?"

"I don't know." She covered her mouth with her hands. "Excuse-moi, Phillippe."

She took the Bible and went inside. I thumbed through the pages of the journal, and landed on a page that said Prayer for Phillippe's future.

> *Dear God, I pray Your protection over my son.*
> *I know this woman he is with isn't Your*
> *best for him. It is my desire that he return*
> *to You and allow You to bless him the way*
> *You have blessed me. Father God, I know*
> *he desires more, but he won't get more*
> *until he lets You in. I pray You will keep*
> *him safe, and that he opens his spirit and*

*heart to You and that good thing You have
for him. I know the woman You have for
him is a good woman like his mother…a
genuine helpmate, a partner, a precious
jewel known only by him. Amen.*

Oh, my God. This is dated a month before he died.

CHAPTER TEN

Gabriella

The pounding on the front door was so loud it resonated up to the second floor. Whoever is assaulting the door better have a good reason for disturbing my quiet time. I climbed out of the tub, put on my robe and ran down the stairs. I stopped at the door, got on my tip toes and looked out the peephole. I stepped away from the door, and then went back to the peephole to confirm what I saw. What the crap! I stood still trying to collect my thoughts, then realized I was only wearing my robe. I pulled it closed, tied the belt tighter, and opened the door.

Oh, my God. Standing before me was the ultimate lustful fantasy…a true alpha male raging with anger, but why? He had a dinner meeting, and I was excited about taking a hot bath and getting to bed early. None of this made sense.

"Phillippe…what are you doing here?"

He pulled me to him and crushed his lips against mine. My initial reaction was shock, then it turned into something else. My hands quickly found their way around his neck, pulling him deeper into my space. His warm tongue broke past my closed lips into my mouth, fighting with my tongue for control of this passionate dance. I needed air, and the only air available was from him. I kissed him harder, hoping to steal some air. We stood in the open doorway engaged in a hungry, demanding kiss so intense my body began to shake.

He pressed his body deeper against mine as his hands slid down my back lifting me slightly off the ground. I could feel his body coming alive through the thin fabric of my robe. His obvious arousal pressed against my stomach. He pushed my robe down my shoulder, followed by a gentle bite and I cried out.

His mouth moved across my chest, kissing the top of my cleavage. I could fill my body reacting in a strange way. My breasts felt full and ached, pressed against his hard chest. Every ridge of his large hands was apparent through the thin silk of my robe. I was on fire, and wanted him in a way I had been fighting.

I tried to pull back, but my body wasn't cooperating. I couldn't believe this was happening. Was I about to give myself to Phillippe right here? He dug his hand deep into my hair, pulling my head back as he ravaged my mouth. Then he pushed me inside, slammed the door, picked me up and took me upstairs, never removing his mouth from mine.

He kicked the door to my room open and tossed me onto the bed. I lay mesmerized, as I watched him strip down to his bare coffee colored skin. My eyes traveled the length of him, and I gasped at what I saw. He's even more beautiful naked. I instantly went from excited to terrified. How was I suppose to…my God, he's incredible in every sense of the word. I swallowed hard, remembering my Aunt Niki's words. Everything on him was large.

He approached the bed without hesitation, and the moonlight bounced off his beautiful coffee colored skin. He glistened like one of the paintings I saw in Paris. He climbed into bed next to me and took my mouth, kissing me so hard I felt it deep in my core. His hand slid inside my robe, grazing my breasts before traveling down the front of my stomach stopping to pull open the belt of my robe. He pulled the fabric of my robe back and his mouth moved down my neck kissing a path to the wet spot between my breasts. My heart was racing, anticipating his next touch. He eased his large hand up the inside of my hot thigh and…

"Gabby…Gabby…Gabby!"

I shot up. "What!"

"Wake up, baby."

"What?" I looked around, and then at myself.

"You're soaking wet. Are you okay?" my mother asked. "Baby, you're burning up. Are you okay?"

"Uhm…" I swallowed hard.

"That was some dream."

"Dream?"

"I heard you screaming downstairs."

"Screaming?"

"Yes. It sounded like someone was attacking you."

Someone was attacking me alright. "Uhm…," I rubbed my neck.

She went into the bathroom and came back with a glass of water. "Here, drink this."

"Merci." I took a few sips of water and exhaled.

"Is everything okay?" She stroked my hair.

"Yeah, I guess I was a lot more tired than I thought."

"I guess so. Are you hungry?"

"Uhm…not really. I think I'll take a shower and…"

"You took a bath when you got home, remember?"

"I did?"

"Are you sure you're okay?"

"I'm fine Mom." I sipped my water.

"Do you want to talk about it?"

I almost choked. "No, no, no…I'm fine. Uhm, you know what, maybe I should eat a little something."

She started towards the door. "I'll make you something and…"

"I'll be right down."

She stopped in the open doorway. "Are you sure you're okay?"

"Yes, Mommy. I'm going to toss some water on my face, put on some dry pajamas, and I'll be right down."

"Okay." She walked out and closed the door.

What the crap! Where did that come from?

Phillippe

"Have you ever kissed a woman so hard it seemed like she was having…you know…" I wiped my face.

I couldn't believe I was embarrassed to ask this. Being with Gabriella has really impacted my life. In the past, I had no problem talking to Tony about the women I was dating. Now, I find myself being very private, protective, not of me, but Gabriella. I want that side of her that she shares with me to remain private. However, right now, I'm vexed about something that happened and I need my best friend's advice.

"What?"

"You're going to make me say it?"

"Yep." He sipped his drink.

"When Gabriella and I were in Paris, and again last night, I could have sworn…Gabriella and I were having a good time, you know. Things were getting a little hot, and all of a sudden she started moaning."

"That doesn't mean…"

"Wait. We kept kissing and the moans got deeper and she was getting a little aggressive. Her body was, uhm…the last time I felt a woman's body react that way, she was on the verge of an orgasm."

He spit out his drink. "What?"

"She was on the verge of…"

"I heard you the first time. Are you sure?"

"This is why I'm asking. I've never kissed a woman who reacted that way. And we weren't in bed or somewhere rolling around naked."

"You don't have to explain." He wiped his face. "Sweet, little Gabriella?"

"Sweet, little Gabriella was on the verge of exploding right there on the sofa behind a kiss."

He shook his head, smiling. "Are you sure? You know it's been a while for you, and everything is magnified when you ain't getting any."

"Tell me about it, but yes." I finished my drink. "If we were to…I don't know if, what am I saying. If we made love, it would probably be incredible and much better than I imagined."

Tony nodded his head. "You could always take your grandfather up on his offer."

"What, marry her so I can become CEO? No."

"Why not?"

"A better job shouldn't be the reason to get married."

"It shouldn't?"

"No. And for the record, I'm still trying to convince my grandfather to change his mind."

"And if you don't?"

"In case you forgot, I have a company of my own to run."

"I'm very well aware of that. However…"

"I know what my grandfather wants. But I'm not going to let him push me into something."

"Uh-huh."

"What's that supposed to mean?"

"Nothing." He sipped his drink.

"I know you. That meant something."

"Okay, let's see. You took Gabriella on a business trip to one of the most romantic cities in the world, and put her up in your apartment."

"That doesn't…"

He held up his finger. "You could have put her in the guest apartment downstairs or another room in the hotel, but you didn't. You let her stay in your home. Something you've never done before. You took her on a shopping spree… introduced her to your aunt…."

"Her meeting Aunt Hilarie was a coincidence."

"Okay, I'll give you that one. Oh, let's not forget you told Cameron to personally handle her at Brockman's and to use your discount."

"That…"

"You and I both know the only people that use your discount are family. Oh yeah, and my favorite confirming fact of all…"

"What?"

"You became celibate. Gave up all booty."

"Are you finished?"

"One last thing."

"What?"

"When are you going to admit you're in love with her?" I exhaled, opened my desk drawer, pulled out the small black box and placed it on the desk. "What's that?"

"The answer to your question. Open it."

He picked up the small black box and opened the lid. "Damn. I guess it's safe to say you're in love with her or, that's one hell of a promise ring." He closed the box and pushed it back to me. "When did you get that?"

"Paris."

"That was only a few weeks after you guys agreed to do whatever it is you're doing. Wait a minute... what else happened in Paris?"

CHAPTER ELEVEN

Gabriella

My phone started vibrating. I looked at the jumping device and read the message. I got up, walked over to the door and knocked.

"Come in."

I pushed the door to the side, walked inside and pulled the door closed behind me. "I received a message to call your girlfriend."

"That's correct." Phillippe looked at his watch as he walked towards me. "According to my watch, we are officially off the clock." He stopped in front of me. My heart began to race, and I felt that strange tingle I get when Phillippe and I are alone.

"That's true. However, I have a report to complete for my boss."

"Well, I'm exercising my authority."

"Your authority?"

"Yes." He slipped his hands around my waist, pulled me close and kissed my neck.

"Phillippe…" He moved his lips up my neck to my cheek. "Uhm…" He pulled me closer and covered my mouth with his. and I quickly gave in to his kiss. I slipped my hands around his neck and we stood in the middle of his office locked in a deep embrace. My mind drifted to the dream I had, and I quickly pulled back.

"What's wrong?"

"I uhm, I really need to finish that report." I started to walk away and he grabbed my hand.

"What's going on?"

"Nothing. I just need to finish that report."

He led me over to the sofa and we sat down. "Talk to me."

"What do you want to know?"

He leaned back and his shocked look was apparent. "What do I want to know? I want to know why you're acting so strange."

"I'm not acting—"

"Gabriella, I know better. What's going on?"

I closed my eyes and rubbed my forehead. I looked at him, trying to find the words to answer his question. "I uhm…I haven't been sleeping well."

"You haven't?"

"No."

"What's going on? Why aren't you sleeping?"

"I've been having these dreams."

"Dreams or nightmares?"

"Considering I'm not sleeping, I'd say they're nightmares."

"Come here." He pulled me over onto his lap, rubbing my back. "Tell me what's going on."

I exhaled. "I've been having these dreams that are uhm…intense."

"Intense?"

"Yeah. They uhm…"

"Close your eyes and just spit it out."

"I dreamt that you had come to my house and took me up to my room and we…"

"What?"

I thought I could get away with skipping over a few parts, but no. He wanted to hear the whole thing. "In my dream, I was taking a bath and went downstairs to see who was pounding on the door. When I looked out the peephole, it was you." I recounted the dream and watched his face for a reaction.

"So you had a sex dream about me."

"What? Where did that come from?" I half smiled.

"You just described a very detailed sex dream. How was I?" he smiled.

"I don't know."

"You don't know?"

"My mother woke me up."

"Your mother interrupted us?"

"No, she woke me up. Apparently, I was screaming very loud."

"Really? Then I guess I was good." He teased.

I playfully socked him. "I don't know about that."

He kissed me on the cheek. "Mon Amour, it's clear this is symbolic of something."

"Like what?"

"I would venture to say, it was about me meeting your family."

"I don't think so."

"Think about it. I went to your house, demanding entry."

I covered my mouth. "Oh, my God."

"Your mother had to wake you up before we could…"

"Oh, my God. You're right."

"I think once I meet your family, the dreams will stop."

———

As much as I don't want to admit that Phillippe is right, the time has come for him to meet my family. God help us. My mother is going to tear Phillippe to shreds.

Right now, my only saving grace is that she hasn't been able to find out anything about him on the internet. His lack of internet exposure is also his biggest flaw.

She thinks he has something to hide, and that's why he has no web presence. I say his lack of exposure is the result of a lot of money. It takes a lot of money to disappear in plain sight, or a friend in a secret government agency. It sounds farfetched, but it's not impossible.

"God help me get through this meeting."

I have been trying to convince myself my father's words don't mean anything. Unfortunately, there's no one remotely interested in that lie. In fact, the people that are close to me and now, those that aren't even in this realm, know what I'm trying to deny. I'm in love.

I can't believe it either. Every time I look in the mirror, or read my father's prayer journal, or allow that still voice to speak, the same phrase comes up. "You're in love with her." For a while, I tried to pretend I didn't know what **her** the voice was talking about. But, I can't deny that either. I'm in love with Gabriella. I think the reason I'm fighting it is because it's a foreign feeling for me.

I'm no saint. In spite of my upbringing, I've been…let's just say, I found it very easy to embrace my French heritage. Yes, I've been with quite a few women. However, I never loved any of them, not even Chantal, and I was considering marrying her. Looking back on the debris of that relationship, I'm wondering why I was willing to settle.

She didn't love me. It's for sure I didn't love her. Yet, I was doing everything I could think of to convince her to stay. I can't believe how grateful I am for my grandfather's meddling. If he hadn't strongly suggested it was time for me to step in and take over Morgan Grant, I would have locked up my life with a woman who only saw me as a mediocre man with a fat wallet. I know she said she admired me. But the night we broke up, thanks to the very expensive wine, she let her true feelings shine. She didn't want me without the powerful job.

If she only knew the truth about my grandfather's offer.

Every morning, when I sit down and read my father's journal, I'm plagued by his words

I pray You send him a wife like his mother.

I know he wasn't talking about Chantal. She was the complete opposite of my mother. However, Gabriella and my mother are a lot alike. I thought my mother's lack of interest or non-interest in my father's wealth was because she came from a similar background. To a degree it was. After reading my father's words, I see he faced the same challenge as me. She didn't care about the money. All she cared about was his character, his heart, and his spirit.

He wrote that he never knew or understood love until he opened himself up to her. Once he let his walls down and shared who he really was deep down, his feelings for her were more powerful than any sexual experience he had ever had.

Now, I understand something he said to me when I brought Chantal home to meet them. He pulled me to the side and asked, "Does she make you see the man God destined you to be?" I blew him off. I wasn't trying to hear a sermon. However, when I'm with Gabriella, I understand his question. She makes me see who I was destined to be.

———

I can't believe I overslept. That's a joke. I think I got twenty minutes of sleep, or something that resembled sleep. The Gabriella dreams were already bad. But now I have my father and the words of his journal being lived out in my subconscious. I need sleep. My body and mind are exhausted. I could always break things off with Gabriella, and hope for a good night's sleep. But that's a joke. Then I would be up all night kicking myself for letting the perfect woman go.

I walked into my office, sat down, opened my father's journal and began reading.

> *I cannot believe I've lasted as long as I have. I made an agreement with Elizabeth which I never expected to have to live out this long. When she confessed how old-fashioned she is, I was startled. In this modern age, I was shocked to discover the woman I fell in love with is still a virgin.*

That was almost as shocking as her pronouncement that she was prepared to walk away from me, if I couldn't respect her decision.

Funny, she used the word respect. I have nothing but respect for her. I see a future with her and I am willing to do something I never have…court a woman by her rules. I sense the payoff will far exceed any temporary false satisfaction. God, I'm trusting You with my heart and pray You guide me in pursuit of this amazing woman. Amen.

Wow. I got a chill. It was like having my father right there with me. To know he chose to make the same decision I did is mind blowing. I sipped my coffee and continued reading.

I did not think I was going to physically survive this dating paradigm Elizabeth presented me. The first couple of months were horrendous. I'm not sure which was worse, the illicit thoughts or my intense desire for her. The intense kisses, subtle glances and gentle touches help. However, it is the dreams I am having a problem with. Those curves and lips plague both my conscious and unconscious mind. Some of the dreams are so real that I have woken up thinking she was lying next to me, only to discover, I'm alone.

I have tried everything, but nothing works. I have resolved myself to the simple fact that she is in my blood and there's only one way to purge her and get the rest I deserve. Come tomorrow, I will get the sleep I long for.

What the crap! How could he just leave it like that. I stood up and started pacing and stopped in front of the floor-to-ceiling window, and did something I hadn't done in years.

"Father God, I need Your help."

CHAPTER TWELVE

Gabriella

Seattle is finally on track which means we are settling into a level four stress zone instead of a level twelve. I actually saw Phillippe and Tony smile. Today is the perfect day to brooch the subject of meeting my family.

I tapped on the door and Phillippe looked up at me. "May I come in?"

"Mon Amour, of course." Phillippe walked over, slipped his hands around my waist and kissed me. The intensity was way more than we agreed upon at work, but it was exactly what I needed. I gave into the kiss and wrapped my hands around his neck, pulling him closer to me. My body was starting to heat up and tingle. He kissed me harder, and it began to feel like the first time we kissed. His hands slid down my back and cupped my behind. I could barely breathe. Suddenly, I heard a deep moan pass from Phillippe to me. I was done. His lips moved across my cheek to my ear.

"I really needed to kiss you."

"Me too."

He closed the door, took my hand and led me over to the sofa in the corner of his office. We sat down and picked up where we left off. I couldn't believe we were in his office carrying on like two horny teenagers. We never kissed like this at work. That was part of our agreement. Not even when we knew there was no one else in the building…we are usually the first ones in the office and often the last ones to leave. But it was only five thirty and there were plenty of people floating around the building.

Phillippe's hands were everywhere. I was pinned against the corner of the sofa with his hard body pressed against mine. In my mind I knew if anyone walked in it would be difficult to explain. However, with all the tension and stress we had been experiencing, it felt good to let loose.

He slowly pulled back, and I looked at him through half opened eyes. Man, he's sexy and smells so good. He has no idea how many times I considered laying down my beliefs and…man, I bet he would make my first time memorable. As Phillippe was pressed against me, I remembered my aunt Niki's words. "Niecy, look at his hands and feet. If they're large, chances are, so is everything else." A chill ran through my body. I looked at Phillippe's hand as he stroked the side of my face, and his thigh wasn't the only large, firm body part pressing against my thigh. I swallowed hard.

"Someone could walk in." I smiled.

He brushed a stray curl off my forehead. "And what would they see?"

"The president sexually harassing his assistant."

"You would have to be protesting for it to be harassment, and I don't see you protesting." He smiled.

I bit the corner of my lip and smiled. "Help me," I said softly.

"What was that?"

"My protest."

"Maybe I am the one being harassed."

"You're on top of me."

"But your hands are around my neck and my hands…"

"Shut up and kiss me again."

"I think that's harassment." He pecked me on the lips. "Do you want to come over for dinner tonight?"

I looked into his eyes. He seemed calm. Now was the time to ask him. I brushed the side of his face. "How would you like to have dinner with my family?"

"Tonight?"

I playfully socked him. "No." Then I thought about his answer. "Why not tonight? You don't have anything on your calendar."

"Yes I do."

"Did you forget I keep your calendar?"

"But you don't keep the one for my girlfriend."

I sat up a little. "You don't have a calendar for me."

He sat up. "Yes, I do."

"No, you don't. You're just saying that, because…"

He stood up, helped me up, we adjusted our clothes and walked over to his desk and he pulled out a small black lizard covered book. He opened it up and handed it to me. I read through the days, noting all the things we had done. He slipped his hands around my waist and pulled me to his chest. Leaning over my shoulder. "Go to today."

I turned the page and under today he had a simple note. Dinner and a movie with Gabriella at home. Must leave work early tonight. I turned to face him. "So what are you cooking?"

"Baked ziti."

"What's the movie?"

"Your choice."

I can't believe I agreed to meet Gabriella's family. What's even more difficult to believe is the way she conned me good. She came over with those dangerous lips, and I never stood a chance. Now I'm going to meet the family.

God help me.

CHAPTER THIRTEEN

Gabriella

I sat in the car as long as I could before getting out and going inside to face the music. Phillippe said I could stay over in one of the corporate apartments, but I knew my mother would have a crap fit. I don't need her freaking out just when I'm about to grant her wish. Phillippe needs to meet her without any added strikes.

"Miss Townsend, is there a problem?" Marcos asked.

I met his gaze in the rearview mirror. "I'm about to go in there and tell my mother I want her to meet Phillippe."

He smiled at me. "Oh."

"She thinks he's…well, she's not…Phillippe isn't exactly at the top of her favorite people list."

He smiled. "Miss Townsend…"

"Marcos, after all these months, I think it's safe for you to call me Gabriella."

"Little Miss…"

I smiled at him. "Baby steps."

"I've known Mr. Marchant, Phillippe for a while, and I think your mother will be very impressed."

"You do?"

"Of course I do. You like him don't you?"

I felt a huge smile rise on my face. "Yes."

"If your mother is anything like you, she will like him as well." He got out of the car, walked around, and opened my door. "It's been my experience, the boyfriend that parents make pre-conceived negative judgments about is usually the one they end up liking, a lot." He extended his hand and helped me out of the car. He took my bag out of the car, closed the door, and walked me to the front door.

"So you think she'll like him?"

He handed my bag to me. "I do."

I exhaled. "Thank you, Marcos."

"It has been my pleasure."

"Are you going somewhere, I mean that goodbye sounded permanent."

"In a way it is. Once Phillippe meets your family, he'll be the one driving you home from that point on."

"But I'll still see you."

"Yes, you will. I have enjoyed being your escort."

I kissed him on the cheek. "Thank you."

"You're welcome." He waited until I opened the door. "Good night. I'll see you in the morning."

"Good night."

I walked inside and closed the door. I stood in the foyer and let the quiet surround me. I looked around and knew that in just a short time, my life would never be the same. I knew my mother would approach this meeting like a general going into battle.

Phillippe

I stood on the porch trying not to hyperventilate. I tried to get Tony to come with me, but he gave me some weak excuse about a prior commitment. What good is a wing man when he won't fly with you on one of the most important flights of your life.

Gabriella said it was a simple family brunch. However, my nerves said otherwise. I asked what her mother was serving so I could bring wine, but she didn't know. I did the next best thing and had a mixed case of wine, and three dozen yellow roses delivered to her parents. She texted me they were impressed, although her mother tried to hide her delight at the roses.

I took a deep breath, and rang the door bell. God, please let Gabriella answer the door.

A few moments later, the door opened. I looked ahead and instead of the beautiful sexy woman that's been plaguing my dreams, it was a slightly older version in a simple white cotton dress. The woman looked like an older version of Gabriella. If this is her mother, Gabriella is going to be stunning when she reaches her mother's age.

I took my sunglasses off and extended my hand to her. "Hello, I'm Phillippe."

"Oh, damn."

"Excusez moi?"

"Mommy," a familiar voice called out. "I told you I would get the door."

I looked past Mrs. Townsend, and saw Gabriella walking towards the door. We were at a standstill. Gabriella finally came to my rescue. So far, this was not going well.

"Vivi…" a masculine voice called out.

"Excuse me."

She quickly brushed past Gabriella. "Mommy…"

"Vivi." The voice called out again.

"Gabby, your father is calling me."

"Did you at least speak to Phillippe?"

She turned around. "Welcome to our home." She turned and quickly hurried away.

Gabriella looked shocked at her mother's behavior. And to be honest, so was I. "Come in."

I stepped inside and she closed the door.

She gently kissed me. We discussed not being too affectionate this afternoon. I didn't need another strike against me. Although, one of Gabriella's deep kisses would be just the sedative I need to get me through this afternoon.

"I'm sorry about that."

"That's okay." I looked at her and the white jeans she was wearing were making this meeting even more difficult. "Great minds."

"What?"

"Your jeans."

She looked down, then at me and smiled. "Oh. Great minds." She took my hand and we ducked into the hall next to the kitchen. "Okay. I need to brief you."

I looked around to make sure no one was around and crushed my lips against hers. At first she tried to resist, but then she gave in. I wrapped her in my arms and slid my hands down her back and pulled her closer. Every one of her curves locked against my body. Her signature parfum traveled up my nose and I was intoxicated. With one kiss, she relaxed me enough to face the barrage of questions that were likely to be thrown at me. I slowly pulled back, and those gorgeous dark eyes slowly looked up at me, and I remembered why I agreed to this meeting. "You were saying?" I brushed the side of her face.

"Uhm…my mother invited my Aunt Niki and Uncle Jimmy. Aunt Niki is my mother's younger sister, and Uncle Jimmy is her husband."

"Aunt Jimmy and Uncle Niki."

"What? No."

I smiled, kissed her again and stroked her arm. "Just teasing you. Aunt Niki and Uncle Jimmy. Calm down, Mon Amour."

"Definitely no French."

I whispered in her ear, "J'avais l'impression que tu l'as aimé quand je te parlais en Français?"

She swallowed hard and cleared her throat. "You know I like everything you do that's French, but no speaking French in front of my family." She smiled and patted my chest.

"So French kissing you in front of them is fine?"

"What? No." She playfully socked me. "Phillippe…s'il the plait…" she sang.

"I thought you said no French?" I grazed her lips with the tip of my tongue.

"Phillippe…" Her pouting and pleading was reminiscent of a sexy French woman.

"Oui, mademoiselle." I kissed her neck and she hummed.

"My family might think you're being rude or arrogant if you start speaking French. And no kissing."

"No French." I kissed her again. "And no kissing." I nibbled her ear.

"Phillippe…behave…"

"Oui, mademoiselle." I kissed her neck and she hummed.

"We better get out there." She stepped out of my grasp, lowered her head, shook the beautiful mass of curls and quickly raised her head up.

"No fair."

"Comment?"

"I'm trying to forget I want to ravage your mouth, but it's a little difficult when you're doing things like that."

She smiled. "Behave."

"I'm trying."

She took my hand and we started towards the patio. She stopped at the door and turned around. "Oh, I told them we weren't staying for dessert. So no matter how much they insist, we aren't staying."

"Pourquoi ?"

"Why? Because I'm desperate to pick up where we left off in the hall." She winked.

I had my orders and if I behave, I get to spend the rest of the afternoon with her wrapped in my arms ravaging those beautiful lips. "Oui, mademoiselle."

We walked out to the patio and all eyes were on us. "Everyone, this is Phillippe."

I swallowed hard and looked at the four sets of eyes staring back at me. This was going to be more difficult than standing before the board telling them I was trimming the fat until the company got healthy.

Phillippe is my worst nightmare come to life. Oh, my God. There's no way this relationship is going to end well. What does a man like that want with my sweet baby girl? Look at him. He's seen things, done things…he's…

"Hey, Vivi."

I invited my sister for support and help probing. Unfortunately, she hasn't taken her eyes off Phillippe since he stepped onto the patio.

"Yes, Niki."

She followed me into the kitchen. "First off, nice wine."

"He sent it."

"Who?"

"Him," I pointed to the man hugged up against my sweet baby girl.

"So that's Gabby's boyfriend slash boss?" She smiled.

"Yes Niki."

"He's the one she went to Paris with?"

"Yes, Niki." She started laughing and shaking her head.

"What?"

"Nothing." She sipped her wine. "Way to go, niecy."

"What's that supposed to mean?"

She walked over to the other side of the counter. "Now I understand the dream."

I forgot I had told her about waking Gabby up from her dream. The one where she was screaming and writhing up and down on the bed. As much as I don't want to admit it, I know she was having one hell of a sex dream about that man. I couldn't look at my sister, because I knew we were thinking the same thing. "Understand what?"

"That my niece was having a hot sex dream about him."

"That's absurd." I continued getting the food ready to go out to the table.

"Did you look at that man?"

"He's a boy."

"Are we looking at the same person, because that is a full grown man." She shook her head. "My, my, my. I'd get Jimmy a pair of white jeans if he could fill 'em out like that."

"Niki?"

"What?"

"Niki, I…"

She walked around the counter, wrapped her arm around my shoulder and turned me around to face the window. Phillippe was so close to Gabriella, they appeared to be locked at the hip. How dare he put his arm around her waist. That's my baby. My sweet innocent baby girl, not some worldly grown woman.

"Look at him." He had taken his jacket off and it was worse than I imagined. "Girl, do you see that behind? Those shoulders? His back is massive and solid. Oh man, and his skin! His skin is incredible! It's like looking at rich, black coffee. Ooo, I just got a chill."

"How do you know he's solid?"

"I checked him out when he walked out here. I saw his chest peeking out from his shirt. That's all muscle."

"Niki!"

"What? And those thighs. Uhm…uhm…uhm…" She patted her chest. "Girl, I bet he could bust a watermelon in half with those big, solid thighs." She took a long sip of her wine. "I know you saw his guns."

"Yes, he has a nice build."

She stepped to the side and looked at me with a furrowed brow. "A nice build? Girl, our husbands have nice builds…well, yours does. Jimmy is working on either a keg, or he's two months pregnant."

I laughed. "Niki…"

"What? It's the truth." She sipped her wine. "Phillippe on the other hand…I gotta admit, I'm a little jealous of Gabby right now. Did you see his hands and feet?"

"I don't see it lasting."

"Obviously you didn't see them in the hall."

I put my knife down. "What happened in the hall?" She had a devilish smile on her face. "Niki…"

"Let's just say if Jimmy kissed me like that before we left home, we wouldn't be spending the afternoon with you and Jerry."

"What?"

"The way they were going at it. And the French. I don't know what he said, but it put a smile on her face."

"Gabby would never…"

"What, make out with her hot, French boyfriend? You need to get your head out of the sand." She turned her gaze back to the patio. "He's a fine catch, and if I have anything to do with it, Gabby is riding this all the way to the finish line."

"Finish line?"

"Marriage."

"No more wine for you." I reached for her glass.

"Stop it." She swatted my hand. "You mean to tell me you wouldn't want him for a son-in-law?"

I thought about her words. Sure, he was attractive and my grandchildren would be beautiful, but I still didn't know anything about this man with a body that should be outlawed. "They just started dating."

"Well, I'll tell you this. It's just a matter of time before he breaks open her cookie jar."

I almost dropped the bowl of corn salad. "What did you say?"

"I said, it's just a matter of time before she gives it up to him."

"I think that's the most asinine thing you've said today."

"Second to you saying he has a nice build? Please…"

"I know Gabriella."

She tapped me on the shoulder. "This is me you're talking to. Do I need to remind you of what happened between you and Jerry?"

"Damn." I dropped my head.

"That's right. Memories, like the corners of your mind," she sang.

"Shut up."

"Okay, now I get it. That's why you've been trippin'. You're remembering what happened with you and Jerry. Well, my dear, if Gabby doesn't have sex with that hot piece of dark chocolate, it will only be by the grace of God. If it were me, Phillippe would have had my knickers on day one."

"Gabby's not me, and she's definitely not you."

We looked out the window at them on the patio. They looked very comfortable with each other. I saw the subtle glances, the gentle touching, the whispering, him brushing her hair back. They looked like lovers.

"That's true, she's not us. But let's be real, neither of us ever had a man that looked like that." She topped off her wine and sipped. "I'm telling you, sis, your sweet little baby girl is probably going to give up the cookies to a man with thighs like solid marble pillars. And from the looks of his large beautiful body, it's going to be a mix of pain and pleasure." She smiled.

"Damn." I snatched her glass and finished it in one gulp.

CHAPTER FOURTEEN

Gabriella

I know Phillippe made plans for us after brunch, but after that tense brunch, I really wanted to be alone. I was afraid to speak, thinking my thoughts about brunch would come pouring out like a flood gate.

He reached over, lifted my hand and kissed it. "What's on your mind?"

Crap! I have two choices, either lie and say nothing or tell the truth about my feelings and thoughts about brunch. I was grateful for my sunglasses so he couldn't read the look on my face. I inhaled and shifted a little, hoping to avoid lying. "Uhm…"

He squeezed my hand. "Brunch wasn't as bad as I thought it would be."

Was he at the same brunch I was, because the tension level was insane. "Is that what you think?"

"Mon Amour, I'm sorry, I tried to be…"

"It wasn't you. It was my mother." I still couldn't look at him. "I don't know why she was so…"

"Rude…insolent…distant…cold…"

I turned to face him. "Really?"

"I'm sorry, baby, but she greeted me by saying 'Oh, damn.'"

"She didn't!" It was worse than I had imagined. "Are you sure you heard her correctly?"

"Oui."

He pulled over to the curb, turned the car off, and removed his sunglasses. He's incredible looking. Every time I look at him, I wonder what I did that God felt I deserved this gorgeous man. I looked at him and he removed my sunglasses. He leaned in and gently pressed his lips against mine and a heat surge ran the length of my body. When he pulled back, I slowly opened my eyes and looked at him through half opened eyes.

"Uhm…"

"I don't want you worrying about me and your mother."

"But I want you two to get along."

He stroked the side of my face. "We will."

"How? Because after what I experienced today, that doesn't seem likely."

"I am going to do whatever I have to to fix this."

"You would do that?"

He lifted my chin. "Yes."

I bit my bottom lip and kept blinking, hoping to push the tears back, but I lost the fight. He smiled and the tears came down. He pulled me to him and I cried like a baby.

"Mon Amour, shhh…shhh…don't cry."

"B-but, but i-it's…"

"It's all going to work out." He rubbed my back. "I promise."

I pulled back and looked at him. "H-how?"

"I don't know. But I promise I will fix things with your mother." He took his handkerchief and dabbed my wet cheeks. "Please stop crying."

"O-okay." I sniffled.

———

I took a shower, put my robe on, picked up my glass of wine and sat in the window seat thinking about my relationship with Phillippe. I like the person I am when I'm with him. I know our relationship is a little unorthodox, but I'm not the first woman to date their boss.

I know my mother thinks I'm naive or a cliché, but I'm not. I'm a grown woman more than capable of being in this relationship. I don't think it's love but strong infatuation. I'm not even sure if I would be interested in something more serious from him. Even is that was what I wanted, it's too soon to make that determination.

All I know is I'm going to enjoy my time with Phillippe

it for as long as it lasts. However, Phillippe's pledge to rectify things with my mother, gives me reason to think he might be more serious than I thought.

Knock…knock…knock…

"Yes…"

"Gabby baby, it's me. May I come in?"

I exhaled. I really wasn't in the mood to hear my mother expound on the many things she doesn't like about Phillippe. But it's better to get it over with now, so I can get some rest.

"Yes." I looked across the room at the door and watched as she entered. Looking at her, you would never know that today she had displayed a rude side I have never seen. She closed the door and walked over and sat on the side of the bed across from me.

"How was your evening?"

Like she really cares. "I wasn't feeling well, so we made it an early evening."

"What's wrong, can I get you anything?"

"No, I'll be fine." I sipped some wine.

We sat in silence a little while staring out the window at the clear dark sky. "Uhm…I want to apologize for my behavior at brunch."

"It's Phillippe you should be apologizing to." I turned to face her.

"I know, and I will."

"I don't understand you Mommy."

"I don't understand me either."

"What?"

"I was rude to Phillippe and that's not acceptable, and it's not me."

"He…"

She held her hand up. "Let me finish, and then if you're still angry, we will deal with it." She exhaled. "Phillippe is a nice man. He wasn't exactly the type of…I mean, you never dated much so I wasn't that concerned about the young boys that came to pick you up for dances or church functions. Probably, because I knew them or their families. But, this man is a stranger. Someone neither your father or I know, and I think that's what scares me."

"I don't get it."

"This is me letting go and trusting your judgment."

"You don't think I'm capable of choosing a suitable boyfriend?"

"That's not what I said. How can I say this?" She stood up and paced a little, and then sat at the end of the window seat. "I think it scares me to see the type of man you're attracted to."

"What?"

"I always imagined the first serious relationship you would have, or the first boy you introduced your father and I to, would be a little more, uhm, simple looking."

"Simple looking?"

"You know, like that boy you dated in college." I started laughing. "What was his name?"

"Are you talking about Todd Elliott?"

"That's him. Whatever happened to him?"

"I don't know." I sipped more wine.

"I was expecting someone like him."

"So you don't like Phillippe because of the way he looks?"

"I didn't say that. I was hoping you were exaggerating his looks."

"I told you he was tall, dark and very handsome."

"In my defense, you said something similar about what's his name…" She was snapping her fingers.

"Todd."

"Thank you."

"No, I recall saying he was tall and a nice guy."

"I wasn't expecting…he looks like he just stepped off the pages of a magazine. My God, Gabby, that's not a young man, but a grown ass man who has seen the world."

"Excuse me?"

"Did I say that out loud?"

"Yes."

"I'm sorry, it's just, he's not what I was expecting."

"For the record, Phillippe, is only a few years older than I am, and I like the way he looks."

"Clearly."

"What's that supposed to mean?"

"I was just expecting something different." She turned and looked out the window. "Look, I know you want me to agree with your decision to be involved with this man, but I can't sign off on it."

"Why not?"

She clasped her hands. "I don't…he's just too slick…too smooth…I…"

"He's done nothing inappropriate."

She turned. "I know that's what you said."

"Oh, my God, you don't believe me."

"I didn't say that. It's just…he seems…that's a man that has experienced life and you…"

"I can't believe we're back on the naïve thing. Yes, I haven't dated a lot, but neither had you when you and Daddy got together."

"That's true, but your father wasn't flying me all over the world and…"

"And what, treating me nice, like Daddy does you."

"I can't help but think this is all a high stakes game of seduction and once he seduces you…"

"I don't believe you. I told you, we aren't sleeping together."

"I know."

"Don't you trust me?"

"I trust you, but I also know how easy it is to be persuaded to do things when there are so many sweet temptations around."

"Temptations?"

"Yes…shopping sprees in Paris, weekend trips on private planes, luxury suites, expensive dinners and…"

"Yes, he bought me some clothes for work functions."

"Don't insult my intelligence."

"What?"

"Work functions? Who needs a Chanel suit and cocktail dress for work. And don't even get me started on the lingerie."

"Yes, those things were gifts, but…"

"It's clear we aren't going to see eye to eye on Phillippe."

"No, we aren't."

"Just promise me you'll be careful. I don't want you so caught up in the fantasy, that you don't see what's really going on."

"What's really going? What are you talking about?"

"You need to ask yourself, what does a man like Phillippe want with a young girl who hasn't experienced life?"

"Maybe that's what he wants…someone who hasn't been jaded by all the trappings he can provide. When we're together, I like the person I am. He's exposed me to so much."

"That's what I'm afraid of."

"Excuse me?"

"Nothing." She got up, walked over, lifted up my chin and brushed my hair back. "You're my sweet baby girl, and I want you to be careful. Promise me, if you don't feel comfortable about something Phillippe says or does, that you'll talk to me?"

I exhaled. "Yes."

She kissed me on the forehead. "Your Aunt Niki said she's a little jealous of you." She started towards the door.

"Why?"

"She said you struck boyfriend gold." She smiled. "I agree with her that he's very handsome. Well, actually she said he looks like he could bust a watermelon in half with his thighs." We laughed.

"Mommy, she didn't?"

"You know your aunt."

"She said it."

"She also said, your Uncle Jimmy, should thank you, because looking at Phillippe, put her in a good mood."

"Oh, my God." I laughed.

She opened the door. "Get some sleep, we don't want to be late for church in the morning." She stopped in the doorway. "You should invite Phillippe to come with us sometime."

"I'll think about it. When he's in town he usually spends Sundays with his mother and grandfather."

"Maybe they would like to join us."

"I'll think about it. Thank you."

"Love you, goodnight."

"Love you, too. Goodnight."

I got off the elevator, looked up and saw my best friend sitting on the sofa in my living room, drinking a glass of wine.

"Wine…not your usual beverage of choice."

"I'm trying to be more civilized."

"What's her name?"

"What makes you think I'm changing because…okay… you're right, but it's a little soon."

I took my jacket off and placed it on the back of the sofa. "Good for you."

"I take it from your call asking me to meet you here, brunch didn't go well."

"Well would have been good." I sat down in the chair next to the sofa, and poured myself a glass of wine. The long sip was good, but to be honest, right now something a little stronger would have been better. "I was hoping when I got there, Gabriella was going to answer the door. Instead, it was her mother."

"Okay, so…"

"On a side note," I took another sip. "Mrs. Townsend is stunning. Wow. Gabriella is going to be incredible looking when she reaches that age."

"I know, her mother blew me away when I first met her."

"It's genetic, because I met her mother's sister."

"And?"

"It was like looking at Gabriella age before my eyes. The curves on those women are unbelievable." I sipped my wine. "How is it even possible one family could…"

"What happened with the mother?"

"She opened the door and said, 'Oh, damn.'"

"What? You must have heard her wrong."

"No. She opened the door, looked me up and down and uttered those two words and nothing else." I sipped my wine.

"You've got to be kidding?"

"No. She didn't say anything again until Gabriella showed up."

"Oh, man."

"Then, her father politely told me he would reserve his thoughts about me, until later."

"This isn't good."

"Once he spoke his piece, he and I were good the rest of the afternoon. Later, he pulled me to the side and commended me for the contract I gave Gabriella."

"What contract?"

That's right, I never told Tony about our agreement. "In order to alleviate some of Gabriella's stress, I told her if we break up, she wouldn't lose her job. If she no longer wanted to be on my team, I would promote her to another division."

"Are you insane?"

"No. It was the only way I…"

"And you put this in writing?"

"Yes. Garrett and Mr. Townsend, and now you, are the only people that know about our arrangement."

"Are you sure about that?"

"Yes. If her mother knew, then maybe she wouldn't be so against me."

"Or, she could try and break you two up."

"You make this sound like some modern day version of Romeo and Juliette. We aren't talking about feuding families. We are talking about an overprotective mother."

"If that's the case, then you need to win over the mother."

"How?"

"I don't know, but it's obvious she doesn't like you. You need to find out why and deal with it. Could be, you remind of her an ex."

I thought back to something my father wrote in his journal.

"I went to her parents and asked what they were looking for in a son-in-law."

Could it be that simple? "I think you're right. I'll invite her to lunch."

———

I picked up my phone and pressed the one number I needed to call before turning in for the evening. I stood in front of the window overlooking the city, waiting for the call to connect.

"Bonjour." Her voice was soft and music to my ears. I love hearing her speak French. It's very soothing and sexy.

"Bonsoir. I wanted to check on you before going to bed."

"Merci."

"How did things go after I took you home?"

"Can we not discuss it."

"Pourquoi?"

"Parceque…"

"Pourquoi, parceque…?"

"Phillippe, s'il the plaît, I don't want to…"

"Je suis désolé…I don't want to upset you." There was a

long pause. "How do you feel about spending the afternoon with me? We can have brunch and visit some galleries, or we can take a drive and have a picnic."

"I don't recall seeing that in your calendar," she teased.

"Funny. I just wrote it down."

"Isn't tomorrow your day with your mother and grandfather?"

"I can see them in the morning."

"I don't want you to change your plans just for me. It's important that you see your family."

"True, but spending time with you is just as important."

"I'll agree to a picnic on one condition."

"Name it."

"No talk about what happened today?"

Like I want to relive that disastrous meeting. "I can do that. Text me when you get home."

"Okay. Bonne nuit."

"Bonne nuit." I pressed the button ending the call. I sat on the side of the bed staring at her face on the phone. She is definitely worth all the changes I'm making.

CHAPTER FIFTEEN

Gabriella

"How was church today?"

Phillippe caught me off guard. I wiped my mouth and looked at him with a slight smile. "It was good."

"What about your class?" He brushed my hair behind my ear. "You mean my Sunday school class?"

"Oui."

"They were excited to see me." I sipped my wine. "You remembered I teach Sunday school?"

"Of course. Come here." I moved across the blanket to his side and he wrapped his arm around me. "I was thinking, what if I arranged for a private tour at a local artists loft or gallery?"

"What?"

"Or, better yet, maybe you could bring them to my office and show them my collection."

"You would do that?"

"Oui. I want to share in the things that interest you. I am as passionate about art as you, and this is something we can do together."

Let me talk with the parents, and I'll let you know." I kissed him. "Merci, Bébé." I nestled into his side. "How was your morning with your family?"

"It was good. We had a nice visit. My mother wants to know when she can meet you."

"What did you say?"

"I told her it was too soon."

"Merci."

"You don't want to meet my moth——-you know what, let's not talk about parents and meetings. Agreed?"

"Agreed."

He lifted my chin and kissed me. "There's something I need to talk to you about."

"What?" I placed a strawberry in his mouth and watched him chew. God, he has incredibly sexy lips. And those dimples.

"That's good." He swallowed and I kissed him. "Are you trying to distract me?"

I kissed him again. "Maybe."

"Our work schedule is about to get crazier. In fact, we need to go to Seattle on Wednesday for a couple of days."

"Okay."

"There's…one of the perks of your job, is an apartment in the city."

"What?"

"One of the perks to being my assistant, is an apartment."

"Is this another gift, because…"

He brushed the side of my arm. "No. I'm serious. It was set up way before I took the position. I think it was so the assistant would be available at a moment's notice for the President."

"I don't…"

"Hear me out. If you stayed in the city, it would be a lot less stressful for you."

"I'm not…"

"Yes, you are. I see it in your face. You're fine the first couple of days, and as the week goes…I know the combination of the hours and the commute are getting to you."

"It's not like I'm driving. Marcos is…"

"He's told me that before you leave the garage, you're asleep."

"Snitch." I looked away and he turned my face back to him.

"He did the right thing by telling me. Why didn't you tell me that it's a little much for you?"

"It's not, really. I mean, I don't want to not see you, but on the nights we eat dinner and go back to the office, I'm…"

"That's exactly why I want you to take the apartment.

Not only will you get a little more rest, but it will allow us to see more of each other."

"Where's the apartment?"

"It's a floor below mine."

"I thought you said this wasn't a gift?"

"It's not."

"What other employees live in the building?"

"Tony, Marcos, Gil and his wife, the pilots and the other flight crew, several of the vice-presidents and the corporate physician and head nurse."

"Oh. I thought…"

"You thought what?"

"Never mind." I smiled.

"We have an agreement. I'm not doing this so I can get you into bed."

"I know. I just thought you were trying to give me… never mind."

"Although, you're staying in the apartment, you're responsible for the monthly maintenance fee."

"What?"

"Everyone on my team living in the building only pays a monthly maintenance fee based on the size of their apartment."

"How much?"

"Meet with the manager and she'll go over everything with you. If you agree to the terms, you can move in when we get back."

"That soon?"

"Yes." He kissed me. "I really think it would be the best thing for you work-wise and for our relationship."

"I'll think about it."

"Mon Amour, if it makes you feel better, only stay there during the week, and go back to your parents on the weekend."

"That's an option."

"But I hope you will make it a full-time arrangement. I really want to get to know you and…do you know the most time we spend together is when we are on the road?"

"That's not true."

"Yes, it is. I want to get to know you away from work."

"Me, too."

"Then it's settled."

"I guess we're going to be neighbors."

"Oui."

This is a good idea. That's what I told myself before I called and arranged this meeting. I repeated those words again after she confirmed our meeting, and I've been saying them every day since then. If Gabriella knew what I was doing, I think first, she would be angry, then she would be happy. I know how important it is to her that her mother and I get along, so I am going to do whatever I have to to give her what she wants.

I can do this, I can make this woman like me.

I pulled up to the curb, turned off the car and sat still. I tossed my head back, closed my eyes and did something that had now become my new normal.

I hope I didn't make a mistake requesting this meeting with Mrs. Townsend. I don't know why there is so much animosity, but I really care about Gabriella, and I know how important it is to her that her mother and I get along.

God, please give me the right words to say, and help me to keep my cool. Amen.

I got out of the car, adjusted my clothes and closed the door. I walked around the car and headed up the walk way. I took a deep breath and rang the doorbell.

The door opened and there she was, my girlfriend's mother. "Hello, Mrs. Townsend."

"Hello, Phillippe." She smiled. "Come in."

We are already off to a much better start. "Thank you."

I stepped inside and stood to the side waiting for her to lead the way. She closed the door and I followed her. I tried not to stare, but it was like watching Gabriella walk in front of me, with a little less wiggle in her hips. I wiped my forehead and tried pushing thoughts of Gabriella out of my mind as much as I could.

"I know you offered to meet in the city, but I thought we would be more comfortable with some privacy."

"I agree."

"Have a seat." I pulled her chair out and helped her get seated. "Thank you."

"You're welcome." I walked over to the other chair and sat down.

"I thought we'd keep it simple." I looked at the nice meal she had on the table…poached salmon, sautéed spinach and roasted potatoes.

"Thank you. It looks delicious. Gabriella said cooking is your therapy."

"I never thought of it that way, but I guess she's right." She placed her napkin in her lap. "Before we start," she bowed her head and said grace. Another thing I have grown accustomed to as a result of dining with Gabriella.

"Amen," we said in unison.

"Help yourself."

"Thank you." I fixed my plate and I was able to get a couple of bites in before she started with the questions.

"Phillippe," she wiped her mouth. "I'm glad you wanted to meet."

"You are?"

"Yes, I owe you an apology for my behavior the first time we met."

"Apology accepted."

She put another forkful of food into her mouth and chewed. I followed her lead. She swallowed, wiped her mouth, and the main event started.

"With that said, I want to know what your end game is with my daughter?"

"Excuse me?"

"Why my child?"

I wiped my mouth. "Gabriella is not a child."

"She's my baby."

"I'm not sure what it is you want me to say."

"You're a very mature, somewhat older man than my daughter."

I think she just called me old. "I don't mean to be rude, but I am not that much older than Gabriella."

"Let's put age aside. You've experienced life, and she's just getting started."

"I'm aware of that." I sat up straighter. "Madame, I think I know what you want to know."

"You do?"

"Yes. Gabriella and I are not sleeping together."

"I know that."

"Of course, she would probably tell you if we were."

"Before meeting you, I would have said yes. However, I don't think that's so any more."

"Excusez-moi?"

"That right there…the French."

"Pardon. When I get excited or confused, I have a tendency to switch languages."

"My daughter came back from her first trip to Paris and she's speaking French, and looks like something out of a French movie. What did you do to her?"

"I didn't do anything to her. All I did was expose her to my culture."

"And that's what scares me."

"I'm trying to follow you, but I don't know what you're…"

"When my daughter told me she finally got her dream job, I was excited. Then she told me who she was going to be working for. I did what any other mother would do. I went to the internet, but I couldn't find out anything about you. Why is that?"

Oh crap! She and Gabriella are more alike than I had imagined. I refrained from making any kind of movement. If she is as observant as I suspect, she would quickly read something into the slightest body change. "What do you want to know?"

"Who are you? How did you get here? And, why my daughter?"

"Is that it?"

"What's going to happen to my daughter once you've grown tired of playing with her?"

That question hurt the most. I am not playing with Gabriella. I have a very large and expensive diamond ring in my safe that would answer that question. "I do not appreciate being insulted."

"Insulted?"

"Oui…yes, in a matter of four simple questions, you have accused me of constructing a very sophisticated plan of seduction that will end in breaking your daughter's heart, and her losing her job. Not to mention you have concocted some nefarious preconceived idea of what kind of man I am, and that I am only interested in taking Gabriella's virginity."

"I apologize if I insulted you, that wasn't my intention."

"I'm not so sure it wasn't."

"And yet, you haven't answered any of my questions."

I wiped my mouth, folded my napkin and placed it on the table next to my plate. "I am the only child of Francois and Elizabeth Marchant. I was born in Paris. Because my mother is part American, my family divided our time between France and the United States. I earned both my undergraduate and graduate degrees from Stanford. I have never been married or engaged, and I do not have any children. Yes, I have been involved with a few women. However, that is in the past. I am dating your daughter because I like her. She is unlike any other woman I have ever met or been involved with. Her energy, honesty, compassion, zest for life and faith intrigue me. As for the details of our relationship, what goes on between Gabriella and myself, is none of yours or anyone else's business. Not that it will assuage your concerns, I am not playing a game with your daughter. I am doing what any man with half a brain would do who met her. I am getting to know her." I stood up and adjusted my jacket. "I would say it has been a pleasure. Unfortunately, the only thing that has been pleasant was the food. Thank you for lunch." I started toward the door.

"So, how long have you been in love with my daughter?"

I stopped and turned around. She played her trump card, and asked the one question I wasn't ready to answer.

The way Phillippe read me answered every question I had about him and his relationship with Gabriella. As hard as it was for me to believe, this young man was in love with my daughter, and prepared to do something about it.

I was fine when it seemed like Gabby's infatuation was one sided. But looking at the reaction on Phillippe's face confirms what I have long suspected. This isn't an infatuation, but love.

Oh crap! What's even worse, my sister might be right.

The End

Thank You

HERE'S A LITTLE MORE

Thank You

HERE'S A LITTLE MORE

THAN YOU for reading THE GOOD GIRL Part Deux! I hope you enjoyed the second part of Gabriella and Phillippe's story. They are just getting started.

Here's a little taste of what happens next in THE GOOD GIRL Part Trois.

Gabriella

I slapped the snooze button on my phone. I needed more time. My family stayed longer than I expected last night.

Nine minutes later when the alarm dinged again, I picked up the phone and tried to make out the time. It took several blinking attempts for my eyes to focus. That couldn't be correct. I put the phone back on the chest and stretched my arms above my head. "Thank you God for this day."

I climbed out of bed and padded along the path to the bathroom. I emptied my bladder and returned to the vanity. The reflection in the mirror in no way resembled the beauty Phillippe was expecting to see in thirty minutes. I really shouldn't have hit the snooze button, because it's going to take some time to wrangle my hair into some sort of style. I can't believe I forgot to tie it up.

I hopped into the shower got dressed and prepared to fight with my hair. I looked at my reflection and decided my hair wasn't worth the hassle. I pulled it up into a top knot.

"Hair done."

I washed my face, put on some serum, moisturizer, bronzer, mascara, lip gloss and checked my appearance in the mirror. *Not bad for a rush mini glam job.* I started toward the door and went back to spray some parfum. *Now, I'm good.*

I headed down the hall and stopped to check on Adam. I poked my head into the guest room and he was out cold. I quietly closed the door.

I was a little nervous for Adam to meet Phillippe. I really wanted them to develop their own relationship. That sounded like I'm hoping things with Phillippe escalate. Aren't they though? I mean, we're going on vacation together and he did say I had stolen his heart. *Get a grip Gabby. That doesn't mean what you think.*

I walked into the kitchen. First things first, coffee. I heated up some water, filled the press with coffee and added the hot water. I looked inside the refrigerator. There were a lot of options. *On my God. This is the first time I'm cooking for my boyfriend.* I felt a full on panic attack coming. I started pacing and shaking my hands. This isn't how I planned it. I was supposed to plan a menu with my mother and do a test before hand…okay, I can do this. It's only breakfast. I stopped pacing, exhaled and walked over to my refrigerator. I opened the door and looked at the sea of food waiting to be turned into a meal suitable for my restaurateur boyfriend.

Ding Dong…Ding Dong…Ding Dong…

I froze for a few beats, then walked over to the door… stopped…exhaled…grabbed the knob and opened the door. I felt my mouth turn up into a smile. All the anxiety I felt was gone.

"Good morning."

"Bonjour."

I stepped back as he entered. He closed the door, scooped me up into his massive arms and took possession of my mouth in a hard passionate kiss. I slipped my arms around his neck giving in to the kiss. The feel of his tongue exploring and searching my mouth was exciting.

He pushed me against the wall kissing me harder… sucking and pulling my lip as his hands squeezed my behind and pressed me against him. His obvious excitement was pressed against my belly. I don't recall him being this excited before. This neighbor thing had its advantages.

He pulled back breathing hard. God he smelled good. I looked up at those sexy dark brown eyes that were almost black. I sucked on my bottom lip and I could taste him. I looked at his mouth and he was now wearing my nude lip gloss.

"I missed you," he said in that deep sexy voice that sent a jolt to my core.

"Moi aussi." I smiled.

"Stop teasing me."

"How am I teasing you?" I smiled.

"You know I love hearing you speak French." He gently grabbed my bottom lip between his sucking.

I moaned and pulled him closer. I wasn't sure what came over me, but it was like I couldn't get enough of him.

He moved his mouth across my cheek, down my neck, sucking. The feel of his hot mouth on me, made my blood boil. I started to shake and I could barely breathe. I was grateful Phillippe was holding me up. He drove his tongue deeper inside my mouth and the tingly sensation grew more intense. He had kissed me like this once before, and it scared and excited me.

He slowly removed his mouth and pulled back. I rested

my head against the wall, opened my eyes and was greeted by his gorgeous smile and sexy dimples. I swallowed and tried to get some air into my lungs.

"Uhm, what do you want for breakfast?"

He locked eyes with me as if he were looking into my soul. Man, my boyfriend is hot. That hot liquid I felt the other day racing through my body was back and gathered in a new place. Talk about welcome to the neighborhood.

"I thought that's what we were doing."

I sucked on my bottom lip and patted his chest. "Behave yourself."

"I'll try." He stroked the side of my face and pecked my lips. "Where's your brother?"

"Asleep."

"No, I'm not."

There were no words for the level of my embarrassment. Phillippe and I pulled apart and turned to see my brother standing with his arms folded across his chest. *Oh crap. Not the way I wanted Adam to meet Phillippe.* I adjusted my clothes and stepped to Phillippe's side.

"I thought you were sleeping."

"I was." At that moment, he was channeling my mother's judgmental look.

I looked at Phillippe and then at Adam. "Phillippe Marchant this is my brother Adam Townsend."

Adam stepped to Phillippe and they shook hands. "Bonjour."

"Hello. So you're the reason my mother is freakin' out."

"Adam…" I was mortified.

"What? I'm not into guys, and right now I'm a little excited."

"Adam…I'm sorry Bébé, he's got more Aunt Niki than me."

"No problem." He smiled and kissed me on the forehead. "It's good to meet you. Gia talks about you quite often."

"Gia?" Adam looked at me and smirked.

"Shut up," I whispered.

"What do you want to eat?" Phillippe walked into the kitchen.

"He cooks?" Adam whispered.

"Yes." I continued into the kitchen. "I was about to make breakfast, but wasn't sure what to make."

Phillippe opened the refrigerator door. "How does everyone feel about French toast?"

"Bébé, I can whip up something," I insisted.

He turned to face me and grabbed my shoulders. "Mon amour, let me and after breakfast, Adam and I will help you finish unpacking."

I looked up and was sucked in by that face. "Okay."

———

"Gabs, I've only spent a little time with him, but I like him."

"You do?" I felt relief. I care what my family thinks about Phillippe, but ultimately my relationship is my business. It's nice knowing my brother likes him.

"Yes. I mean, oui." We laughed.

"Is someone becoming bi-lingual?" I teased.

"I better, seeing I'm probably getting a bi-lingual brother-in-law."

"What?" My eyes got wide at his statement. He only said what I have pushed back in my mind.

"Gabs, you can lie to yourself all you want, but he's playing the long game."

"He's just…you think so?"

"Yes." He sipped his wine.

I dragged my finger around the rim of my glass. "He uhm…"

"Is this another thing I have to take to the grave?"

I smiled. "Yes or you can tell afterwards."

"Did he propose?" He put some popcorn into his mouth.

"What…no. Why would you say that?"

"It's obvious."

"No. He uhm…we…we're going on vacation together."

"Uh huh." He ate more popcorn.

"Did you hear what I said?"

"Yes."

"Why aren't you surprised?"

He finished his wine and placed the glass on the table. "Because I watched him with you. This guy is serious. How do you feel about him?"

"I'm not…I think it could be love, but I've never been in love, so how would I know if what I feel is love or just strong affection?"

"I can't answer that for you. Only you know the answer. However, if you ask me do I think you're in love, based on what I observed and the way you talk about him, yeah, I think you're in love."

"I think about him constantly and he's stalking me in my sleep." My face felt warm.

"From the sound of it, you've got it bad. Talk to Mom."

"Really?" I said with a hint of sarcasm.

"Okay then, talk to Aunt Niki."

"The lesser of two evils." We laughed.

"Aunt Niki is cool. I know she can be a little frank, but that's what you need. Unlike Mom, she sees us as adults. I had a situation and she helped me."

"Excuse me?"

"Talk to her. You can trust her Gabs. I mean Gia." He smiled.

"I'll think about it."

He stood up and stretched. "Well, I'm going to turn in. I'm meeting my future brother-in-law at the gym in the morning."

"Really?"

"Yes. Did you see his guns? I gotta get in shape to keep up with my future brother-in-law. So tomorrow is day one of my new workout plan."

He extended his hand to me to help me stand up.

"Thank you, sir." I shook out my neck.

"Are you turning in or…," he smirked.

"I'm going up to Phillippe's for a bit."

"Uh-huh."

"What?" I smiled.

"Good night."

"Bonne nuit."

The soft sound of Nina Simone filled the space. I felt strange.…at ease, but anxious. I enjoyed spending the day with Gabriella and her brother. It felt comfortable.

I know I'm on borrowed time. I thought my grandfather would have come around by now, but he hasn't.

His wanting me to get married and take over Morgan Grant wasn't going as I planned. I shouldn't have to have a wife to be CEO. My grandfather's thinking is antiquated. Unless there's another reason behind his demand.

If I give in to him on this, he'll never see me as qualified to take over. I need a plan that will work to my advantage and not his.

I want to introduce Gia to my mother, but I have to do it when my grandfather isn't around. I don't want him saying anything about my job and family before I tell her myself. Tony was right, I should have said something a while ago.

Ding…Ding…Ding…

I didn't need to turn around because I saw her reflection in the large window. I watched her walk towards me and my body got hard. I really need to be careful. This morning, I think if we had been alone, that morning kiss would have turned out a lot differently. I'm determined to go all the way with this relationship and that means playing by Gabriella's rules.

She stopped behind me, eased her delicate hands around my waist, inhaled my shirt and rested her head on my back. I lifted her hand to my mouth and kissed it.

"I could get used to this."

"Me, too." She inhaled. "I love the way you smell."

"And I love how you feel next to me."

"I like the vibe you have going on. Sort of like a speakeasy."

I turned around to face her. This was the face I saw in my dreams. I cupped her face in my hands and it seemed small and fragile. Like I was holding a priceless work of art.

I pressed my lips to hers, slowly pulled back and looked deep into her eyes. This was the perfect time to tell her everything, but I couldn't. It was too soon and I didn't want to scare her. Even worse, I didn't want to lose her.

"You're beautiful."

"You're pretty good looking yourself." She smiled.

I eased my hands around her waist and pulled her closer. "I wasn't expecting to see you tonight."

"Why not?"

"I thought you and Adam would be catching up."

"He turned in. Something about getting up early to meet you in the gym." She smiled. "Merci."

"Pour quoi?"

"For being nice to my brother."

I smiled. "Did I pass?"

"Not that it matters, but yes." She splayed her hands on my chest.

"Oui, it does." I pulled her closer. "It matters because he's your family. Things may be a little strange with your mère, but I see how special your brother is to you." I tucked a stray hair behind her ear.

"True."

"Besides, I need all the allies I can get." He smiled.

"What?"

"We need to settle things with your family, before we take on mine." I kissed her on the forehead, took her hand and we walked towards the sofa and I sat on the back and pulled her in between my legs. "Want to watch a movie or grab a bite?"

She hummed. "Both sound intriguing. I should go so you can get some rest."

"You sure?"

She sucked on the corner of her lip and smiled. "Don't tempt me."

I pulled her closer and caressed her behind. She licked her lips, and started breathing hard. The swell of her breasts was tantalizing. She wanted to be kissed. I kissed her jaw and moved my mouth to her ear. "You sure?" I gently tugged on her ear and her breath caught.

"I uhm…"

I kissed her neck and she tossed her head back and sighed.

"I…I…I need to leave…"she swallowed hard.

I dragged the tip of my finger along her arm and her

skin started to pebble. This exercise in seduction was to tempt her, but it backfired.

I gently kissed her. "You're right. You should go." I stood up, took her hand and escorted her to the elevator. I pressed the button and the elevator doors opened. Another advantage to having a private elevator, immediate access. I held the door open and watched as she boarded. Then I stepped behind her.

"What are you doing?"

I stepped within a breath of her. "I'm escorting you home."

She smiled. "What if someone sees us?"

I stroked the side of her face. "Bébé, the only people on your floor are you and Tony."

"I forgot." She smiled.

The elevator stopped and the doors opened. I took her hand and we walked down to her apartment. "Bonne nuit, mon amour."

"Good night."

I kissed her and watched as she entered her apartment.

———

Read **THE GOOD GIRL Part Trois** now!

About the Author

A California native, novelist Tracy Reed pushes the boundaries of her Christian foundation with her sometimes racy and often fiery tales.

After years of living in the Big Apple, this self proclaimed New Yorker draws from the city's imagination, intrigue, and inspiration to cultivate characters and plot lines who breathe life to the words on every page.

Tracy's passion for beautiful fashion and beautiful men direct her vivid creative power towards not only novels, but short stories, poetry, and podcasts. With something for every attention span.

Tracy Reed's ability to capture an audience is unmatched. Her body of work has been described as a host of stimulating adventures and invigorating expression.

Sign up for Tracy's newsletter:
www.readtracyreed.com/newsletter

Like Tracy Reed on Facebook:
facebook.com/readtracyreed

Join Tracy's Reeders reader group:
readtracyreed.com/tracysreeders

Follow Tracy on Instagram:
instagram.com/readtracyreed

Visit Tracy's website for her current booklist:
www.readtracyreed.com

facebook.com/readtracyreed

twitter.com/readtracyreed

instagram.com/readtracyreed

bookbub.com/authors/tracy-reed

pinterest.com/readtracyreed

Acknowledgments

"Thanks to my friend Cheryl Winborne for giving me her honest opinion on Gabriella and Phillippe's story.

Merci, to my French expert and RWA Buddy, Brenna Aubrey. I really appreciate your patience and help. I hope I corrected the French as you instructed. If not, I'm sorry. I'm stilling learning this beautiful and complicated language.

Thanks to one of the newest members of my author tribe, A.M. Roark for the brilliant cover feedback. It really helped me find the right for Gabriella and Phillippe's story.

As always, thanks to my Editor Jeanne for being so patient with me.